WADE'S WAR

It's 1865 and the Civil War is ending. On their small Missouri farm outlaws murder Wade Tretter's parents. Fourteen-year-old Wade sells the few cattle remaining and heads west to find the killers. After killing two of them in an act of retribution, Wade finds the last two men posing as model citizens in a small Kansas town. How can he beat the odds and bring these powerful men to justice without hurting their new families?

Books by Chet Cunningham in the Linford Western Library:

JIM STEEL No.5: GOLD TRAIN

CHET CUNNINGHAM

WADE'S WAR

Complete and Unabridged

LINFORD
Leicester

First published in Great Britain in 2010 by
Robert Hale Limited, London

First Linford Edition
published 2011
by arrangement with
Robert Hale Limited, London

British Library CIP Data

Cunningham, Chet.
Wade's war.- -(Linford western stories)
1. Parents- -Death- -Fiction
2. Murder- -Fiction.
3. Revenge- -Fiction.
4. Western stories.
5. Large type books.
I. Title II. Series
813.5′4–dc22

ISBN 978–1–4448–0760–8

Published by
F. A. Thorpe (Publishing)
Anstey, Leicestershire

Set by Words & Graphics Ltd.
Anstey, Leicestershire
Printed and bound in Great Britain by
T. J. International Ltd., Padstow, Cornwall

This book is printed on acid-free paper

1

Western Missouri
5 April 1865

Fourteen-year-old Wade Tretter hunkered down in the big bluestem grass twenty yards from the cabin. He stretched out hidden by the tall growth and partridge pea plants as he watched the four horsemen riding toward the small house on their Missouri farm. Just yesterday his pa had warned them about raiders. They were outlaw riders, mostly Rebels, who ravaged the countryside robbing, burning, and killing. They had been raiding in Missouri for two years but hadn't come into this valley.

As he watched the riders, the wonderful smells of summer were all around him. The sharp, greenish tang of the pea plants, the sweet fragrance of the crab-apple blossoms that lifted on the gentle breeze, and the moist earth musk of the just-turned sod in the plowed field.

He saw the darkening clouds in the blue sky and hoped for rain. All the time the riders came closer. He shivered when they rode in close enough for him to make out the rag-tag Rebel uniforms. Three of them wore the Confederate gray shirts and Rebel forage caps. The fourth had on a complete Southern uniform except for the gray cowboy hat. No regular Southern Cavalry had ever been in this area.

He had to stay hidden like his pa said until he knew the men were friendly. Wade fingered the Whitney single-shot rifle he had been using to hunt wild turkeys. The riders were close enough for him to recognize the rifles in the scabbards. They were Henry repeaters, which the North used. How did Southern soldiers get them? If he had to fight them he would get off one shot, maybe two, but then they would cut him to pieces with their repeating rifles.

His pa walked out of the cabin. The four men rode in close and reined up. The rancher waved at them.

'Hi there, strangers,' Howard Tretter said. 'What can I do for you? I'm a farrier. Be glad to check over the shoes and hoofs on your mounts. No charge.'

'You're right, no charge,' one of the mounted men said. Wade watched in stark terror as the rider in the cowboy hat drew a six-gun and fired. The other three Rebs shot at almost the same time and Howard Tretter jolted backwards staring in disbelief, then slammed to the ground. The rancher tried to turn over but collapsed.

Wade knew his pa was dead. He saw his ma rush out of the door and stop. She screamed, then ran back in the house and slammed the door. How could he protect his ma?

He shook his head, totally confused. It had happened so fast. His pa was dead. It took him a few more seconds to realize it, then he beat his fists on the ground and tears rushed from his eyes. Fury flooded him and he wanted to charge the men, firing as he went. But fear froze him where he was. His hands shook as he held the rifle. Sweat beaded his forehead. His mouth went dry and his stomach rumbled. For a second he didn't think he could breathe.

His pa had warned him. 'If any raiders do come here, Wade, and you're out in the garden or the pasture, don't come to the house.'

He flattened lower, concealing himself in the tall grass. He tried to stop his hands from trembling and his teeth from chattering. He'd never seen anyone killed before. He mopped the sweat off his forehead. So far the raiders hadn't seen him. Tears surged up and ran down his cheeks. He brought up the rifle and aimed at the closest rider, but then he lowered the weapon.

No, he had to think. To be smart like his pa had taught him. He had to stay out of sight; otherwise he would die, too. He dropped his head on his arms and sobbed. His pa . . . dead. It was hard to believe. Just two minutes ago his pa had been alive. Now his ma was in danger.

What could he do? First he had to crawl closer so he could hear what they were saying and see what they looked like. He would memorize their faces and forms, burn them into his memory so he never forgot them. He had to get a good description of each killer. He wiped tears out of his eyes and swallowed hard.

The raider with the cowboy hat stared at the house.

'I'm going inside, men, to see what this sodbuster's woman looks like,' the rider in the full uniform said. He swung down, dropped the reins and walked twenty feet to the front door. Wade saw a black patch over his left eye. He tried the door, but it was locked. He stepped back and kicked the door twice before it swung open. The Rebels cheered.

Wade stiffened. His ma. The man was

going after his ma. He had to do something. Shoot the raider? No, then he'd die, too. All he could do was lie there.

The other Rebels laughed. 'Leave some of that loot for the rest of us, Rudy,' one called.

Wade grabbed the name. Rudy. They called the one with the full uniform and cowboy hat Rudy. He repeated the name over and over again. He would never forget it. Closer, he must get closer. He could squirm through this tall grass over to the little stream where it mothered a crooked row of brush, some shagbark hickory and a few young buckeye trees. Then he could crawl along this side of the stream. The brush would give him cover almost to the cabin. He left the rifle and wormed slowly toward the house, trying not to make the tall grass move.

It seemed like it took him an hour to get to the scraggily old crab-apple tree and the red mulberry. But it had been only a few minutes. The house sat fifteen feet across the small stream. He could see the side window but not the front door. He watched through the brush and a heavy growth of switch and Indian grass that hid him. Three of the Confederates lounged outside.

One Reb with a full beard went inside the cabin and came out a few minutes later screeching in delight.

'Lookee here, I got me a Greener double-barreled shotgun and this old Sharps and Hankins rifle. She's a fifty-two caliber and will shoot a mile.'

Wade studied the man. He stood taller than his pa, maybe five ten, and skinny. Brown hair that matched his beard showed when he took off his Rebel cap. He carried his left arm bent a little, like it wouldn't straighten out.

'That long gun won't do you no good when you're punching cattle out there in Kansas,' the shortest man said. Wade watched him. He stood five inches shorter than the bearded one, and maybe 140 pounds. His sleek black hair framed his clean shaven face that looked long and thin, like a bat.

Rudy came out of the house munching on some bread. He walked with a slight limp. The raider's pistol holster hung on his left side. He still had the black patch over his left eye.

'Next to check the loot,' Rudy shouted and the bearded Reb put down the long guns, whooped, and ran into the house.

Wade beat his fists on the ground. He couldn't stop them and not get killed himself. They were murdering outlaw raiders, like Quantrell. These men owed no loyalty to the South.

He concentrated on the last man. He looked older than the others, maybe thirty-five. About the size of the first man, five foot ten and clean shaven except for a full brown moustache. He showed a round face and mousy brown hair, but he was different. He had no left hand, just the empty end of his sleeve.

Wade shivered again watching the killers. He was ashamed that he couldn't protect his mother. It was his duty now that his pa was dead. He shook his head and scowled. As he waited, he listened to the soft gurgling of the small stream as it flowed past. He heard a frog croaking. The humid area next to the creek with its wet-earth smell and the dozens of green growing plants brought a welcome relief from the hot dry April day.

He wiped more wetness from his eyes and swallowed the last of his crying. He lay there agonizing over his mother's fate. They wouldn't kill her too, would they? His pa had told them these raiders seldom left a witness. He wouldn't think about it. His ma had to be all right.

Then he heard shouting from the house. He recognized his ma's voice. A man bellowed in anger and then his mother screamed again and again until the last sound he heard was a whimper. A minute later the bearded Rebel came running out of the house. He carried a knife in his hand and wiped the red blood off it in the grass. It had to be his mother's blood. He felt faint and the sunlight dimmed. He struggled not to lose consciousness. He shook his head and pried his eyes open wide. He had to know what happened.

'Bitch!' the bearded man screamed. 'No woman gonna call me dirty names.'

'So you stuck her?' the smaller man asked.

'Right.'

'So how she gonna cook supper for us now, you stupid wooden head?' Rudy snarled. 'That makes you the cook. Get back in there and find us something to eat. We got to be moving on west.'

'How far we going?' the one-handed man asked.

'You heard me talk about Kansas,' Rudy said. 'There's this Flying W ranch out there in west Kansas. It's a huge outfit and always needs hands. We can get jobs as cowboys. We can bunk down there for a year or so and see if anybody comes hunting us.' Rudy watched the bearded Rebel. 'Come on, knife-man, get back in there and cook us some supper.'

The beard slapped his forage cap on his brown pants leg and scowled. 'I ain't no good cooking.' He looked at Rudy, then moved toward the cabin.

'Captain, you suppose the lawmen gonna be looking for us out there in Kansas?' Rudy, the man with the black eyepatch, asked.

'Not a chance,' the shortest man said. 'Them lawmen out there will have troubles enough without borrowing any from Missouri. Once we get over the border into Kansas we'll be free and clear. That's why I want to get us moving. We got three weeks of hard riding to go.'

Wade caught the word 'captain', and looked at the shorter man. Was he a military captain, or was it just a nickname? He didn't know but he would remember the captain from now on. From his hiding spot by the creek Wade saw smoke come out of the chimney. It blew gently toward him and he caught the tangy bite of the burning buckeye wood. They were getting supper.

He could move back the way he came or stay there. He decided to stay. He was stuck there until it got dark or the men rode away.

He rolled over and took a notebook and stub pencil out of his pocket. For months he had written down descriptions of the different birds he saw. So far he had noted fourteen different ones from red-winged blackbirds to the least bittern. Now he used the empty pages and put down everything he had seen and heard about the four men. He listed Rudy first. He seemed to be in charge. Wade wrote down his appearance, how he talked, what he wore, a total description.

He went from Rudy to the captain, then the bearded man, and last the killer with one hand, noting all the details. By the time the sun had dropped low in the western sky he had it all written. He would remember what these four men looked like until the day he died. He trembled, living again through the shock of seeing his father murdered.

Just before dusk the sun sank behind a cluster of red and deep-crimson clouds on the horizon, then the sun faded and dusk settled in. The cooler air brought the scent of new-mown hay and clover blossoms.

He heard voices as the four men left the house and moved to their horses. They talked for a minute, then mounted, and looked at the house. One asked if they should burn it down.

'Be fun to see it go up in smoke,' Rudy said. 'But if we burn it, somebody might notice, ride over here, and could get on our trail. So we let it be and fade away into the night. Nobody will even know we been here.'

They turned and rode west. Two of them had pillowcases filled with stolen loot tied behind their saddles.

When the raiders were out of sight

Wade ran straight for the cabin. What had happened to his ma? He burst in through the door and the sickening smell of copper hit him in the face. It was the same smell as when they bled out a steer. It had to be his ma's blood. He took a match from the holder near the stove, struck it, and lit a coal-oil lamp. He put the glass chimney on and turned down the wick.

Then he edged into the bedroom. He found her on the bed with knife wounds on her chest and throat and her blood spread all over. He cried as he knelt in front of the bed, sobbing. At last he stopped. He was too old to cry. He was over fourteen. He said a prayer for his ma. She was in heaven with his pa.

He covered her with a blanket and went to look at his father. The farmer lay where he had died. Wade rolled him over on his back and stared through the darkness at his face.

He knelt in front of his pa and tears came again. His pa had been a good man. He said a prayer for his pa and wished him well in heaven. He went inside the cabin that had been his home for the last four years. He sat at the small kitchen table a minute. In three hours his whole life had been dumped upside down. He set his jaw. He knew what he had to do next. He went out to the shed and found a shovel.

★ ★ ★

Two hours later he had finished digging a grave near the mulberry tree. He sat on the pile of dirt, exhausted. He rested for a few minutes before he went back to the cabin.

Later he lowered both his parents into the grave. He had wrapped them in blankets and put them side by side. Then he let the tears come as he filled the hole. He made a wooden cross out of two by fours and pounded it into the ground as a head-marker. He painted on their names and the date, then he took a blanket, his rifle, and went into the brush along the creek to sleep. He didn't want to risk any more Rebel raiders coming to the house.

* * *

The next morning he woke up cold and stiff. He ran back to the house and looked for something to eat. Everything of any value was gone, including most of the food. He found some rolled oats and cooked it in an iron pot on the wood stove. That and an apple served as breakfast. Then he sat down and thought over what he should do next. The little farm had been rented. They had a few chickens, a hog the raiders had missed, one horse and twelve head of cattle down in the far pasture. He'd ride to the Johnson ranch four miles over and see if the owner would buy the cattle. Mr Johnson would give him an honest price for the cows and steers, maybe twenty dollars a head. Then he'd take Betsy, the horse, his dad's kit of farrier tools, and head west.

He found his pa's six-gun and gunbelt in a box under the kitchen wood pile where his pa usually hid it. The raiders had missed it. The weapon was an old Colt Navy revolver, the percussion cap kind for which you had to put the little nipple firing charges on each cylinder. He'd take it along and trade it for one of the new solid cartridge Colt revolvers. Then he'd have to practice with it.

Wade was pleased with his plan. He was old enough to fend for himself. He stood tall for his age, nearly five-feet six. He'd heard about several kids his age who had to go it alone. His pa had trained him to be a farrier. He could work his way West. Most towns didn't have a farrier. Most ranches always needed work done on their mounts' hoofs and shoes.

One of the first things he needed to do was find a good cartridge six-gun he could handle. He set his jaw and headed down to the south pasture where Betsy, his pa's saddle horse, grazed. As soon as he sold the cattle he would ride into Bellview and tell the sheriff about the Rebel raiders and that he'd buried his folks. Then he would head West and he wouldn't stop until he found those four killers.

2

By noon on that first full day after his parents had been murdered, Wade was on his way West. He had talked to the sheriff, who said two other ranches had been attacked that same day and four more people killed. The raiders had got away.

Wade had gone to the general store in town and used some of his $240 of cattle money to buy an outfit for travel. He had a small frying pan and a metal pot, two tin plates, silverware, a pair of tin cups, a box of kitchen matches and what he figured was a week's worth of food: a loaf of bread, a jar of home-made peach preserves, two tins of soup, a half-pound of butter, a quart can of rolled oats, two pounds of potatoes, and half a dozen eggs. He knew nothing about cooking. He would learn.

He passed through a half-dozen small farms. Missouri was mostly farming country, so little need for a farrier. By dusk he figured he had ridden ten miles.

He found a small stream near a grove of fragrant sumac with no farm nearby and made camp. Already he missed his mom's bright smile. She had been such a happy person, always with a kind word and encouraged him in his studies. He was thankful that he could read and write. Hard telling what he'd need to know as he worked West. He was fourteen. All he had to do was ride West, watch for places where he could get work as a farrier and stay alive.

He started a small cooking fire, sliced some potatoes into his skillet and let them fry like his mom used to do. Then when they were done he put in a pair of eggs and with two slices of bread he cut from the loaf, had a good meal. He'd never learned to like coffee, but he figured he should. Next time he got supplies he'd get himself some already ground coffee and find out how to boil it.

Night fell suddenly and he huddled closer to the fire. He'd heard that a traveler should never sleep beside a fire out in the open. The fire was a beacon for other travelers, some of whom might have bad intentions. He pulled the saddle off Betsy. She was a six-year-old mare, a roan chestnut color with speckles of white and gray. She was no speedster, but she was deep-chested and good for a long ride. He brushed her down and tied a long lead on her so she could reach the creek and do some grazing.

Then he put out the fire and rolled out his two blankets that he had tied over the back of the saddle under the foot-long metal box that held his farrier tools. He'd heard that cowboys used their saddles as pillows, but he tried it and didn't like it. He curled up in the blankets. It had been a long and hard day. Leaving the little farm had been the toughest part. Now he'd be in a different place every day.

He blinked back tears thinking about his ma and pa. They were dead and gone. He still had a hard time realizing that. He had to accept it. But he could still hate it.

He took a deep breath, watched Betsy through the faint moonlight where she grazed on the new grass. Then he closed his eyes and went to sleep.

⋆ ⋆ ⋆

The next morning he woke up and for a fraction of a second didn't know where he was. Then the memory of the gunfire came back to him and his ma slashed and stabbed in pools of blood and he felt tears coming. He smashed them down. Big guys don't cry. The time for crying was over. It was time for action.

Pancakes. How had his ma made them? Flour and something. He'd ask at the next general store. He'd need syrup, too. He had two eggs and toasted some bread over the small cooking fire. After a long drink from the stream, he filled the flat saddle canteen and was ready to ride.

* * *

Two hours later he came to a prosperous-looking farm and decided to stop by. He'd never talked to strangers much, but he was going to learn. He decided to be friendly and not say much.

A man walked from the modest house toward a barn, and when he saw Wade riding in he waited for him.

'Morning, sir. My name is Wade and I'm a farrier. Wondered if you had any need of my work?'

The farmer was in his thirties, wore a straw hat and had his blue shirtsleeves rolled up above his elbows. He looked at Wade for a moment and a smile broke through his slight frown.

'Matter of fact, young man, I do have a mare that threw a shoe and the rest of my six head could stand looking over. My name is Nate.' He held up his hand and Wade reached down and shook it. 'You charge much?'

'Fifty cents a shoe. Nothing for the inspection and some minor clean-out work on the hoofs.'

'Sounds reasonable. Got me a dozen shoes or so in a box. Should find one to fit. You got the nails?' Wade nodded. 'Come out to the corral and I'll show you the mare.'

Wade followed the man. He grinned. Found work on his first try. This might not be so hard after all. If he could make a dollar a day with farrier work, he would have enough to buy food with, and maybe stay in a hotel now and then.

The hoofs on the mare needed work. All had grown out and distorted the fit of the shoe. He cleaned out the hoof without the shoe, trimmed down the excess and nailed on the iron. Then he looked at the other front shoe. He called the farmer over.

'The other three shoes are out of place because of the growing hoof. I can trim down the hoofs and the shoes should be OK for another few months. You'll have to watch them. Or I can do the job right and take off the old shoes, trim down the hoofs where they should be and put on new iron.'

The farmer looked at the hoofs. He nodded. 'Yep, you're right. I ain't been watching them close enough. Tell you what. That other front one is worst. You replace that shoe and trim up the two back ones and I'll give you a dollar and a quarter.'

'Deal,' Wade said. He went to work on the other hoof. By the time he was done he heard a bell ring. The farmer came back and checked the hoofs, gave Wade a paper dollar and a silver quarter.

'Good job. I dearly hate to shoe a mount. Much obliged. That's Wanda on the dinner bell. Come up to the house and eat with us.'

'That's kindly of you, sir. I best wash

up first.' They stopped at the well and Nate primed the hand pump with a can of water. He pumped four times, then the pitcher pump gushed water out of the spout with every stroke.

Wade was used to eating dinner. Farm folks needed their strength and a big noon meal was the answer. Today Wanda had fried chicken, mashed potatoes and gravy, fresh baking-powder biscuits, and early green beans from her garden. There was also coffee. Wade took a cup and watched Nate put a spoonful of sugar in his. Wade did the same. It tasted a bit strange, but he drank it. When they were done, he thanked Wanda, shook hands with Nate and asked about other farmers in the area who might need farrier work.

'Old Jake next door is an ornery cuss. Wouldn't bother with him. Beyond him is Shorty Chrisent. He's good folks, but don't have no money to pay you. Farther on I don't know the men too well. Wouldn't hurt to stop and ask.' He grinned. 'Fact is, you should come to a place just before suppertime. That would be a good time to check on work. Maybe get yourself invited into the kitchen for a good meal to boot.' He paused. 'How old are you, son?'

'I'm fifteen.' He lied but wanted to seem older.

'On your own? That's too young. You be careful out there and ride tall in the saddle.'

Wade thanked him and rode westward. He went past two farms and the third he stopped at but they didn't need any farrier work and they didn't invite him to stay for supper. He rode on until dark, then stopped by a creek near some honey locust and put Betsy to graze. He made a small fire and fried half the bacon. One more day and it could spoil. He had slabs of the bread and bacon sandwiches, then opened a tin of applesauce and ate the whole thing. He brushed down Betsy, then at dark he put out the fire and curled up in his blankets. The ground was softer here in the shade by the stream. Still it was lots harder than his bed on the farm. That made him think about his folks again. Why had they been killed? It was a question he would ask the Rebel raiders if he ever found them. That question probably would haunt him for years.

The next morning he came to a small town and stopped in the general store. A woman stood behind the counter. She smiled.

'Good morning. You're new in town. Here to stay or passing through?'

'Heading West,' Wade said. 'I need some supplies and I have a question. What do I need to make pancakes? My ma always used to make them but I didn't watch her.'

'You're on your own, then?'

'Yes, ma'am.'

'Pancakes. You surely do need a recipe. I'll write it down for you. Got a notebook?'

He pulled out the notebook and turned it to a fresh page. She wrote down the ingredients:

1 egg
1 cup of buttermilk or milk
2 tablespoons of butter
1 cup of flour
1 tablespoon of sugar
1 tablespoon of baking powder
½ teaspoon of baking soda
½ teaspoon of salt.

The woman looked up. 'You have a fry pan?'

'Yes, ma'am.'

'You'll need to grease it a bit before you pour in the batter.' She paused. 'You need the makings?

'Yes, ma'am. I have the salt and sugar. How long will eggs keep?'

'Usually not much more than a week. You need some?'

They worked out what he was shy of and she found the smallest tins of baking powder and baking soda. She scooped out two pounds of flour for him and put it in a cloth sack.

'Now, the milk will turn on you in four or five hours on a warm day. Best you get fresh milk the night before and have your hot cakes the next morning.' She frowned. 'Now say you really want some hot cakes and no milk. You can use water. Won't taste quite as good, but it will work. What kind of syrup do you want?'

He bought six more eggs, another loaf of bread and the goods to make flapjacks and a pound of beef jerky. The total cost was just over three dollars. At this rate he was going to go broke just eating. In the morning he'd ask around town about doing some farrier work. He figured there had to be at least 1,000 people there. Biggest settlement he'd come to so far. He rode out of town a half-mile along the creek and made his camp under some tall trees.

The next morning he tried out the flapjack recipe and was delighted. He had four large pancakes and syrup on them and drank the last of the quart of milk.

He had slept in a grove of American sycamores west of town. He cleaned up his breakfast things, repacked and rode back into to town, He reined up in front of the general store. There he tied Betsy to a hitching rail and laid out his farrier tools on the boardwalk. Ten minutes later a rider stopped by.

'You the farrier?'

'Yep.'

'You know your onions?'

'My pa taught me. I do good work.'

'Suppose you prove it to me. I need two new shoes on back of my gelding. He won't take kindly to your messing with his feet. I'll hold him if you think you can do it.'

'I can. Been kicked once or twice, so I'll be careful. Powerful-looking animal. You got the new shoes?'

'Had them in my saddle-bags for a month. Just never got around to putting them on. How much?'

'Fifty cents a shoe.'

'Done. You do him here?'

'Rather lean him up against a building. Over there in the alley.'

By the time he had the two shoes on

the nervous gelding, there was another man asking about him doing some farrier work. He had four more customers before noon and wound up with just over four dollars. He splurged and had a bowl of stew, two slices of toast and then a piece of pie at a small café.

He waited on Main Street for an hour after dinner, but no more customers came, so he bundled up his farrier tools and rode west. So far, so good. Two full days on his own and he had made over seven dollars. Not bad. At this rate he might save up enough to take a stagecoach part of the way.

Soon the ritual of riding into a ranch or a town became routine for him. He'd find out about customers, do all he could, and ride out. In one of the larger towns he stayed a week. Every day he made enough to pay for three meals and his hotel room. Those were the times he considered settling down in one larger town and opening a farrier's shop, or going to work for a blacksmith.

But in the end, he always moved on. The urge to find those men who killed his parents was deep and strong.

One day merged with the next, and then the next. Soon it was winter and he found a reasonable hotel in a town and did enough farrier work to pay his expenses through the cold and snow. With spring he was out and moving West again.

3

Plainsview, Missouri
6 July 1868

Wade Tretter sat on the edge of the boardwalk in the small town of Grovers Corner tossing pebbles at a beetle that was trying to crawl through the inch-thick dust of the street. He had stumbled on the boardwalk and sat down hard. He'd seen dozens of boardwalks during the past three years. He knew the store owners were trying to keep the dirt and mud of the street out of the stores. He was surprised that each merchant built his own boardwalk. That was why he'd stumbled. One boardwalk section in front of one store was six inches higher than the one right beside it.

It had been three years since Wade's folks died, three tough years of growing up, of working his way West as a farrier. He thought about his parents every day, wishing with all his heart that the war had ended a month earlier. It had been tough. But his pa had taught him well. He'd been in a hundred small towns, and at ranches, doing farrier work to stay alive.

He'd stopped in one small ranch and done their horses, and the woman of the place took a liking to him. They had no children and she mothered him all day, bringing him lemonade and just-baked cookies. She had him stay for supper and then asked him to stay over with them for the winter. He had been fifteen by then and was worried about the second winter. So he agreed to stay on the ranch until spring. He'd stayed there for six months, then thanked the family and moved on West. He'd hoarded the $240 he got for the cattle. It was deep in his saddle under a flap he'd riveted down.

He was seventeen now, and had grown to five feet eleven inches tall. He didn't know whether he'd stopped growing or not. His arms and shoulders had developed as he plied his trade with rasp and hammer. His face had filled out and showed a firm jaw, wide-set blue eyes under heavy brows and brown hair that he kept cut short. A two-inch scar showed on his right jaw, the result of his first fist fight when he was sixteen. His work as a farrier kept him lean and strong at 160 pounds.

The black beetle plowed his way through a pile of dust and headed for the wooden supports of the boardwalk. Wade let him go.

Wade stared to the west. He figured he was about twenty miles from the Kansas border. Once over the line he'd start asking questions about the Flying W ranch. The raiders had said it was in western Kansas, so he could have another 350 miles to ride. It made him excited just thinking about it. At last he was going to be able to get some information about the four killers.

The first few months away from

home he'd asked here and there if anyone had seen four men riding west. Some had, but it could have been any four men. Now he counted on that elusive Flying W ranch as the best bet he had to find any of the raiders.

A rider on a sorrel stopped in front of him. 'Hey, you the farrier?' the mounted man asked. 'You the guy who fixed up Brownie's mare with new shoes?'

Wade looked up and nodded.

' 'ppears as how.'

The rider on the sorrel looked to be in his thirties. He had on a high-crowned white hat and wore a brown leather vest over his gray shirt.

'Old Sorry here threw a shoe about a mile back. I can get a new one at the general store if you'll put it on for me. Hate to shoe a horse myself. That's worse than talking with my mother-in-law.' The rider chuckled at his own joke.

Wade stood. 'Yep, I can do it. The other shoes in good shape?'

The man nodded. 'You're right. Lose

one shoe, better look at the other three. How about I ride into that alley and you can check the other shoes?'

Wade pulled his farrier case off the back of his mount and carried it to the alley. The sorrel's right front shoe was loose and badly worn. The other two were in good shape.

Wade lifted the mount's hoof again and the rider measured it with his hand. Then he went to the general store. He came back with a shoe in each hand.

'Found two that should fit good,' he said. 'How much do you charge?'

'Quarter a shoe,' Wade said.

'Not enough. I'll give you a dollar for both of them and be glad I found you.'

'Deal,' Wade said.

He took the shoes and pushed with his shoulder against the sorrel so she put her weight on the other foot, then he lifted her left front leg and checked the new shoe. It would be a good fit. He cleaned the hoof of built-up dirt and some small rocks. It had grown out and needed trimming. That was so the shoe would fit exactly the outside of the hoof. The heel of the hoof must rest on the iron.

He put six nails in his mouth, trimmed the hoof down and tried the shoe. A little more trim and it fit. He pounded in the nails, making sure they came out the sides of the hoof and didn't penetrate into the soft, tender part of the inner hoof. The first shoe went on quickly. Then they turned the animal around and Wade pushed his 160 pounds against Sorry and she leaned against the wall again. Wade pulled off the loose shoe, cleaned and shaped the hoof and shoe and pounded it in place.

'Hear you're new in town,' the rider said.

'Yep, just passing through. On my way to Kansas.'

'They got lots of horses out there.' He handed Wade a silver dollar. 'We could use a full-time farrier here in Plainsview.'

'Not enough horses to make a living,' Wade said. 'I got me some important business out in Kansas.'

The rider mounted his sorrel and nodded at Wade. 'Much obliged for the help. You want to stay we can find enough business for you.'

'Thanks, but I'm on my way in the morning.'

That afternoon Wade took his six-gun and rode out of town a half-mile. He paced off twenty feet, pulled out the used Smith & Wesson hinged-barrel .44 caliber revolver. It had rim fire cartridges so there was no fuss with primers. It held six rounds and he was getting better with it. He wasn't trying to draw it quickly, just to draw and shoot straight. He picked out a tree twenty feet away and fired at it. With the first six rounds he hit the twelve-inch-wide tree only one time. He sighed and reloaded. By the time he had fired thirty times, he was doing better. On the last six shots he hit the tree four times. An old-timer had told him a year ago that shooting straight from the hip was like pointing your finger at your target and squeezing the trigger.

Back in town he bought two more boxes of .44 solid cartridges at the general store and went up to his one luxury in over a month, a real hotel bed.

* * *

In late August 1868 he rode into the settlement of Coletown, Kansas. It had been cattle country for the last fifty miles. He tied up his mount to the hitching rail and looked around. He'd been in dozens of small places like this in the past three years. Most of them were a lot alike. Here there were maybe 300 people. More saloons than stores. He could see one church. More than half the men wore gunbelts with revolvers slung low on their thighs. He lifted his gunbelt off the saddle horn and strapped it on.

When he hit a new town he always bought his provisions from the general store first. He stacked up two pounds of dry beans, a loaf of fresh bread, two cans of tomatoes, two cans of applesauce, and a half-pound slab of bacon. He hadn't seen canned applesauce for a year. He also needed salt and flour, a bottle of syrup, five pounds of good-looking potatoes, and half a dozen eggs. Everything together cost four dollars and twenty cents. The store man was young with red hair and a built-in smile.

'Heading West, I'd figure?' he asked.

'True. Just rode in. You have a farrier in town?'

'Can't say that we do. Old Jim at the livery will do the work but he hates it. You might give him a holler if'n you're a farrier.'

'That I am. Where's the livery?'

Twenty minutes later Wade found Old Jim, and was met with a welcome shout when he learned Wade was a farrier.

'Boy, I can use you. Got me three old nags I can't rent out 'cause they got bad feet. Think they just growed out their hoofs too much and I didn't take care of them. Can you fix them up for me?'

Wade worked until dark. He trimmed and shoed the three horses that had been neglected, and then put rear shoes on two more mares and all four on a prancing solid black gelding. The big horse hated shoeing and Old Jim had to hold the gelding's head and talk to him during the whole shoeing.

By the time Wade finished he'd earned five dollars and twenty-five cents. He went to the only hotel and took a room, washed up, and put on his only clean shirt. He even combed his hair. At the best-looking restaurant in town he splurged and paid fifty cents for a steak dinner with mashed potatoes and gravy, peas and carrots, two big biscuits, and a pot full of strawberry jam. Best food he'd had in two weeks.

The waitress looked to be about his

age. She was short, had shining black hair, a slender figure, and a big friendly smile. She came back twice to check to see if he needed anything else. The last time she lingered.

'You new in town. You gonna be staying?'

'Not unless a whole batch of riders need to have farrier work done,' he said.

'Heard you helped out Old Jim down at the livery.' When he looked up surprise on his face, she shrugged. 'Small town, word gets around fast.' She tarried. 'Well, if you need anything, you just call.'

'I could use a piece of pie. You have any?'

'Cherry, apple and gooseberry.' Her smile came back.

'The gooseberry.'

'Yes, my favorite, coming up.' She watched him a minute, then her smile widened and she turned and hurried away. She brought the pie and had added whipped cream on the top.

'I like it with the whipped cream. Is

that OK?' she asked.

'You bring an extra fork?'

She laughed. 'No, silly. It's just . . . you know.' She shrugged. 'I figured you'd like it too.' Her smile showed through, lighting up her green eyes.

'My ma says I'm too forward sometimes with boys.'

'Like now?'

She laughed and he liked the sound. He hadn't talked with a pretty girl for six months.

'Do you think that I'm too forward?'

'Not at all. Just one person talking to another person. If you sat down beside me and helped me eat the gooseberry pie, that might be forward.'

She pretended to sit beside him, laughed softly, and hurried back to the kitchen.

After his supper, Wade went back to his hotel room. It was small, the mattress lumpy, the mirror cracked, but it would be luxury after a week straight sleeping on the ground.

* * *

A half-hour later he pushed through the no-nonsense door of the First Chance saloon. He usually checked the drinking and gambling establishments in towns, on the off chance he might find out something about the four Rebel raiders. This was the third and best saloon he'd been in so far that night. He'd learned two years ago not to order sarsaparilla in a saloon. That had got him into a nasty fight in one town. Now he ordered a beer and sipped at it as he checked out the men. None of the four he hunted was here. He scowled.

He was about to leave to check another watering hole when he heard something that stopped him.

'Looks like our one-handed gun-fighter has done it again,' a range-rough cowboy at the bar said. The barkeep grunted.

'You best not talk that way when he's around.'

'Don't worry. He's out of town.

Some gent up in Lawton picked a fight with One Hand last night and got himself shot dead before he could clear leather.'

'He's coming back here?'

'Stage driver said he's aiming north toward Topeka. He must have some gunhand business up that way.'

'Now, Harley. You telling me our One Hand is a hired gun? That he goes around killing people for money?'

'No, no, I'd never say that. I did hear you say it though.'

Wade put his beer mug on the counter and headed out of the saloon. Then he stopped. One Hand, a gunfighter. Could that be the one-handed man he hunted? Was this one of the four men he tracked out of Missouri? After the war there must be hundreds of ex-soldiers on both sides with only one hand. Still, it was a chance. He stopped a man just coming in the saloon.

'I hear One Hand is around town a lot. Does he have a stump of a left arm cut off at the wrist?'

The cowboy pushed back his hat. 'You too young to be a marshal so guess it's all right to tell you. Yeah, he has that stump and he gets right mean with it. For two years he swamped out saloons here in town and lived like an outcast behind the general store. Then he found out he could shoot. Man, could he shoot! His left hand gone didn't mean nothing. He got so good he gunned down three young men one after another who thought they were shooters who called him out right here on Main Street.'

'So, he has a reputation?'

'That he does. Nobody around this end of Kansas wants to go up against him.'

'He have another name, before he got to be One Hand?'

The cowboy frowned. 'You sure curious. Think you can beat him?'

'I'm not a gunman. Just curious.'

'Yeah, he had a name, Larch something. Ask Hank over at the

general store. He took care of him those first two years when everybody else treated him like dirt, laughed at him, and played tricks on him. We don't do that anymore.'

Wade thanked the cowboy and went outside into the warm Kansas autumn night air. Larch. He could think of no men named Larch. He hurried up to the general store. The owner was in his sixties, white-headed, and wheezed when he breathed.

'Oh, sure, I know Larch. A poor, wretched soul for a couple of years. Then he found out he was fast on the draw. I never see him any more. But once a month I get an envelope with twenty dollars in it. Say what you want to about Larch Creighton, but he remembers me.'

Wade went back to the hotel. He planned to get to bed early. He ordered three buckets of hot water and had a scrub down in the small bathroom on the first floor. It might be some time before he had this kind of luxury again.

Tomorrow morning he would ride north toward Topeka. He had a name, he had a man who shouldn't be hard to find. He also had a problem. If this Gun Hand Creighton turned out to be one of the four Rebel raiders, how could he go up against a fast-draw killer? But there was no proof that this was the man who had shot his pa. He'd have to wait and see if this was the right man.

Wade was up with the sun and got his gear and his food all packed and ready to travel. He tied his rucksack in back of his saddle along with the farrier tools and checked the restaurant. By his pocket watch it was only 6.30, but the Top Notch restaurant was open. As soon as he sat at one of the small tables, the same pretty girl he'd talked to last night walked up.

'Hi, morning. You're up early. I'm Alice.'

He held out his hand and shook her small white one.

'Good to meet you. Do you have bacon?'

'We have a special: two eggs any style, grilled grated potatoes, toast and coffee, and bacon with a side of flapjacks all for twenty-five cents.'

'Sounds good. I'll take it.'

'Be right up.' She hesitated. 'Why were you asking about One Hand? You don't look old enough to be a lawman.'

'Curiosity. And you're right. News and gossip travels fast in this small town. Make those eggs over easy.' She flashed her best smile and hurried away. Did all the people in town know about his interest in One Hand?

Alice brought the order and stood there a moment, watching him.

'Is it all right?'

'Looks delicious.' He motioned to the chair across the small table.

'Sit down and rest yourself, Alice.'

She frowned. 'Not fair, you know my name but I don't know yours.' She held up her hands. 'I know, I know, it ain't polite or healthy to ask a man's name out here sometimes. But I don't think you're a wanted outlaw on the run.' She sat down. There were no other customers.

He dug into the eggs and bacon and she smiled.

'You have a name?'

'Wade.'

'Wade. I never knew nobody called Wade before.'

He went on eating.

'Saw your mount all loaded up at the rail. You heading out?'

'You ask a lot of questions, don't you?'

'Yep. Always have. Where you heading?'

'North.'

'And you don't talk much at all, do you, Wade?'

A small bell rang from the kitchen area. Alice stood. 'Oh, boy, that's my pa calling. Usually we use that bell when an order is up and ready for me to take out. I ain't put in any more orders.'

'So you're in trouble?'

'Naw, that's my pa back there. He owns the place.' She headed for the kitchen.

Wade watched her walk away. He didn't know much about girls. What he knew he liked. He wanted to know a lot more about Alice. He shook his head. But girls would have to come later. First he was moving West.

He had just finished his meal and he stood up when Alice came back.

'Pa wanted to tell you that the town needs a farrier. He's the mayor here. Says lots of cowboys and town folks could use a farrier and make it worth your time to stay.'

Wade nodded. He smiled watching this small girl being so serious for a change. 'Well, I appreciate it. Thank your pa for me, but I got to move on north and then west.'

'You be coming back this way?'

'Probably not. Be nice to settle down for a bit, but I got to keep moving.'

She shrugged. 'So I probably won't ever see you again?'

'Probably.'

She reached up, kissed him on the cheek, then she quickly stepped back.

'My ma says a cheek kiss is all right, if'n you like the boy.'

He couldn't think of a thing to say. Her smile got bigger, a tear edged out of one eye, and she waved as he walked out the door and across the boardwalk to the hitching rail. Yes, she was something. He wanted to learn a whole lot more about girls.

* * *

By eight o'clock that morning he had ridden five miles north of town on a wagon road that was little more than a worn pair of wheel tracks through the gently rolling plains. Near a small creek he rested under a huge black oak and a smattering of flowering dogwood. The white blossoms reminded him of home. He watched the sky. After spending most of the last three years outdoors, he had learned to read the sky, the clouds, and the winds. Now he saw a scattering of high clouds that was working slowly east.

He let his mount drink her fill at the creek, then headed on north. There was almost no one on the road. Twice he met lone riders heading south. One wagon came toward him, then turned in at a lane that led behind a small rise where he saw smoke coming up, evidently from a ranch house.

Back at the saloon a man had told him it was about fifteen miles almost due north to the next little town and this road would get him there. After that it would be a long, long ride to Topeka. He calculated the odds of One Hand Creighton being the one who had shot down his pa. He figured from what the general store man said that there was a chance this was the right man. But there must have been a thousand men after the war with only one hand. The good thing was he had time to check out this man. A gunman like One Hand would leave a trail of talk, gossip, and probably dead bodies wherever he went.

4

The man with one hand stood at the bar, a bottle of whiskey and a shot glass in front of him. He had ridden into Johnson Creek two hours ago, rented a room at the only hotel, had supper, then found this saloon. He wore a black low-crowned wide-brimmed cowboy hat, a black shirt, string tie, a buttoned black-leather vest, and black pants.

'This better be good whiskey, bar-keep, or it's your scalp.' He stared hard at the man behind the bar. 'What's your name?'

'Jones.'

'No, your given name.'

'That's it, Jones.'

'Well, Jones, this whiskey better be good, like I said.' He lifted the glass and tossed the drink down in one gulp. For a moment he let the taste tingle in his mouth. Then he threw the small glass at the barkeep. He grabbed the whiskey bottle with his good right hand but the burley bartender had lunged for the bottle at the same time and with two hands tore it away from the drinker.

'Easy, mister,' Jones said. He tried to evaluate the man across the mahogany. His eyes were steel-hard blue, his clean-shaven face a mask of fury. His left arm's stump thumped on the bar. The stranger stepped back from the bar and in one fast move drew his six-gun and blasted a round through the four-foot-square mirror behind the bar. Glass flew and heavy pieces of the mirror broke whiskey bottles under the mirror.

The barkeep jumped back, stared at the ruined mirror and the broken bottles, and held up both hands, palms out.

'Hey, take it easy, mister. I've got better whiskey but it costs more.'

'Best whiskey you got,' the man with one hand said. He dropped his six-gun in leather, reached in his pocket and pulled out a twenty-dollar double-eagle gold piece, and dropped it on the polished wood. 'This should cover it and the mirror.'

Jones pulled another whiskey bottle from under the bar, poured a new shot, and left the bottle.

Larch Creighton had felt uneasy all day. Usually he didn't care, but today it had seemed worse. He hadn't had a shoot-out in three days. That bothered him. He had to keep his edge. He'd practice tomorrow morning. Get some kid to throw beer bottles in the air.

He drank the new whiskey and nodded at Jones, who had sweat through his shirt front. He saw the nod and went up the bar.

Larch needed a fight tonight. He checked the men in the place. About half wore guns. One stood at the bar down a ways. Larch poured another shot of whiskey and downed it with a toss of his head, then one more shot, which he sipped as he watched the man down the bar drinking a beer. He had a six-gun on his right hip. Larch moved that way and just as he came to the man, stumbled and jolted into the man's shoulder. They both staggered to stand up.

The drinker at the bar turned, his face red with sudden anger. He saw the furious man behind him and he calmed, then shrugged.

'Sorry, my fault,' he said.

'Yeah, your fault. Why don't you stay out of my way?'

'Sorry. I'm just trying to have a beer.' He turned away.

Larch grabbed him by the shoulder and spun the farmer around. The farmer fell back against the bar. His face had gone pale, his eyes hooded, and sweat beaded on his forehead. 'Said I was sorry.'

'Didn't like the tone of your voice.'

'Sorry. Didn't mean to bump into you.'

'There you go doing it again. You chicken-livered little sidewinder. You've got a weapon. I'm calling you out here and now.'

'I'm not a gunman, I . . . ' The farmer stopped when the other man's head snapped up, fury in his eyes.

'No yellow-bellied excuses.' He screamed the words and all conversation in the bar stopped as everyone watched.

Two men whispered at a suspended poker gamne.

'That guy is One Hand,' the man with two queens showing said. 'Yeah, hear he comes from south a ways,' the man with a four and six on the table said. 'Nobody's ever come close to beating him.'

'I'm calling you out, you coward,' Larch roared. 'Nobody talks to me that way and lives to tell about it.'

The farmer, still leaning against the bar, shook his head. 'Not a chance I'm going against you. Heard about you, One Hand. I won't draw on you. You shoot me if you got to, but we have a good sheriff in this town and he'll have you in jail inside of ten minutes. Unless you want to go up against three men with double-barreled shotguns.'

'Big talker,' Larch sneered. 'Get on your knees and beg.'

The farmer shook his head.

Larch chopped the barrel of his six-gun down on the man's shoulder once, then again, then pushed with his hand and the side of his left arm until the farmer's legs buckled and he went to his knees.

'Now, beg for your life, farmer. Beg me not to kill you.'

The man on his knees looked up and shook his head.

Larch roared in fury and jolted his right knee upward suddenly ramming it into the farmer's chin, snapping his head back and slamming him flat on the floor. He lay there without moving. Larch screamed at him.

'You want more, you stupid lout? Get up and fight me.'

He waited a moment but there was no answer.

Larch stepped up and kicked the

farmer viciously in the side. Three poker tables back the players could hear two ribs break.

'You like that?'

Larch kicked him again.

'That's enough, One Hand,' the barkeep Jones said, his voice barking with authority.

One Hand turned, his right fist hovering over his six-gun.

'Try it, big shot,' Jones said. 'Nobody alive ever drew against an aimed shotgun. You try it and I'll blow you right out the front door.'

Chairs scraped on the wooden floor. Men scurried out of the scatter pattern of the sawed-off shotgun's double aught buck.

Larch stared at the two ugly black muzzles and let his hand drop.

'Easy, barkeep. I'm just havin' some fun with the farmer here. He ain't half dead. No account to get nasty with that Greener.' But the sneer never left Larch's face. 'Pulling down on me with a Greener. No man alive ever done that before.' He shrugged. 'First time for every thing, I reckon.' He looked hard at the barkeep. 'I remember faces real well, you sniveling little bar rag.' He turned his back on the Greener and walked slowly toward the front door. He was almost there when he spun, drawing his Colt as he turned, and fired in one swift fluid movement.

The Greener blasted at almost the same time, but the barman had let his aim drift off the gunman and all but two of the big slugs smashed through the front window, missing One Hand.

The barkeep stared wide-eyed at the miss, then the shotgun fell on the bar and he grabbed his chest. A moment later he slid down behind the bar.

Larch Creighton grinned. He dabbed at a spot of blood on his cheek where a slug had grazed him. 'Oh yeah, there still ain't a man alive who drew down on me with a shotgun. Warned Jones, the little bar rag. You all saw it. I fired in self-defense with an already drawn weapon aimed at my back. No need to call the sheriff. I'll be at the hotel if he wants me.'

He tipped his black hat, dropped his six-gun in the holster, and walked through the front door. Outside, Larch felt the continued rush of emotion. He was ten feet tall. He could lick a pack of wolves single-handed. He could fly over the moon if he just had wings. He had squashed Jones like a bug even when the crazy had a shotgun aimed at him. Oh yeah! No bullet could touch him. He had only been nicked twice by hot lead in all of his encounters. He thought a moment. Seventeen. Jones was number seventeen on the notches of his six-gun. Every one of them had fired a weapon at him.

He angled across the street to the Kansan Hotel. The room clerk behind the front desk was the same feisty little redhead he had noticed before. He liked her looks. Her fiery red hair set his blood pumping, She was alone in the lobby.

'Hey, sweetheart, I need to talk to you.'

'Yes?'

'Why don't you take an hour off and come up to my room?'

'Absolutely not. You are outrageous.'

'You know who I am?'

'Someone I don't like.'

'I'm One Hand, the fastest gun in the West.'

'I'm not impressed. If you don't leave, I'm calling the manager.'

'So call him.' One Hand darted around the end of the high desk and grabbed the woman's arm. 'I told you, we're going up to my room.'

She screamed and he slapped her.

A door burst open at the side of the lobby and a large man holding an axe handle surged toward the desk.

'Phyllis, what's wrong?' He stopped when he saw One Hand. He hesitated. 'She's my wife, mister. Let her go or you'll be in big trouble.'

'Not as much trouble as you are,' One Hand said. He dropped the woman's arm, drew his Colt, and sent two .44 caliber slugs into the manager's chest, slamming him backwards against the wall. He died as he slid slowly to the floor.

The woman cowered against the desk, her eyes wild.

'You killed Wally.'

'Yeah, his problem. Now, you're coming upstairs with me.'

She screamed and flew at him, her fingernails clawing at his face, and her hand found flesh, scraping two raw lines down his right cheek. He had holstered the six-gun. Now he drew a four-inch knife and slashed at the wild woman tearing at him. One knife swing sliced across her arm and she bellowed in pain. The next thrust of the blade hit the side of her throat, severing the carotid artery and blood pulsed out with every heartbeat. Phyllis sagged to the floor, her eyes full of fury and wonder at what had happened so quickly.

One Hand bent and wiped the blade on the woman's dress, pushed it in the sheath, and ran up the stairs to his room. There had been no witnesses to the killings.

It took him ten minutes to get his gear together in his room. Then he walked out the hotel's side door and down to the livery stable where he had put his horse. Nobody was on duty there. He got his mount out of the corral, saddled her, and mounted up. He would be miles up the north road before anyone found the bodies and spread the alarm. Even then they wouldn't know who they were looking for.

The sheriff still might want to talk to him about the barkeep. He would want to be sure it was self-defense. Someone might have seen the hotel killings through the windows. Better move quickly.

He urged the horse forward at a canter. He'd run her at that pace for a mile, then walk her a mile. He should be able to move a good six miles in an hour that way instead of just four walking his horse. He wasn't sure what small town was next on the little-used road but he'd go past it and on north. No sense in stopping too soon and let the news of the killing catch up with him.

Larch Creighton settled in the saddle. He had a long ride ahead of him. He didn't want to be late for his meeting in Wildwood, a small town thirty miles south of Topeka. He had a letter to see a rancher there named Halstead. The rancher had sent along a fifty-dollar bill to encourage him to come up for some gunhand work.

5

Wade rode north along the wagon road that sometimes withered into little more than a horse trail. At the first small settlement he came to, he stopped and talked to the town marshal. The man was about sixty, with a range-weathered face, rheumatism in his knees from sleeping on the ground too much, a soft smile, and a low voice.

'Nope, never seen the gent. Heard of him. He's been getting himself a reputation around these parts. We don't have much in the way of gun play in our town. Lots of farmers, some ranchers, and a few drunks on Saturday night.'

'I hear he's a hard man to miss,' Wade said. 'Thanks anyway for your help.' He stood, shook hands with the marshal, and went outside. It was just after noon. He found a small restaurant and had a bowl of soup and a sandwich. There was no Alice to serve him, just the cook who hadn't shaved for three days. Wade ate and moved on.

The next town proved more helpful. It was ten miles from the last one and Wade found they didn't have a town marshal. He talked to the barkeep at the best saloon in town.

'Yep, he was here. We all know about him. He was mean and nasty, demanded the best of everything. He had lots of cash and paid for everything. Our luck that he didn't kill anybody in town.'

'He say where he was heading?'

'Didn't, but I happened to see him ride out. He was on the wagon road north.'

Wade thanked him, rode out of town five miles and camped beside a little creek for the night. He had sliced ham and fried potatoes for supper. He had never learned to like coffee, so he had water to drink. He put out his small cooking fire and moved with his horse fifty yards away from the spot. He rolled out his blanket and put his head on his saddle for a pillow. Maybe tomorrow he'd find out more about One Hand.

* * *

The next day about noon he rode into Johnson Creek. It was the largest town that he'd found lately. He figured it had over 1,000 people. About a third of the men wore sidearms. He found the county courthouse and the sheriff. The sheriff was a town man, black suit, no sidearm, pale face, soft blue eyes, and a slight twitch in one of them. His voice was easy to listen to and he sounded more like a lawyer than a lawman.

'Yes sir, we know all about One Hand here in Johnson Creek.' The sheriff held out a Wanted poster. 'He was here two days ago and left in a rush at night after killing two men with his gun and a woman with his knife. We've got a Wanted poster out on him with a two-hundred-dollar reward. That's for One Hand, dead or alive.'

Wade looked at the poster. There was a good description of Larch, plus the note that he usually wore all black and his left hand had been amputated at the wrist.

'Can I have one of these?' Wade asked.

'You bet. Nobody else has seemed much interested.'

'His real name is Larch Creighton.'

'You don't say.' The sheriff wrote it down. 'From what folks say he headed north. Will at the livery woke up when he saddled up. Will said he didn't pay for the keep and rode out on the north road.'

Wade went back to his horse and moved north. One Hand was two days ahead of him. That meant about forty miles. Two days. He had to make up some time. He would ride twelve hours. He should be able to make forty miles that way. Gain twenty.

* * *

The next three small towns he came to knew about One Hand, but he hadn't killed anyone in any of them. He found out at Cherry Hill that the gunman had spent the night there and most of the next day. Good, now he was only one day ahead.

Wade stopped at the next town and found out where he could buy a quart of milk. The general store owner beamed. He was in his forties, had a wild mop of brown hair, wore spectacles, and had a gimpy right leg. He laughed softly when Wade asked for milk.

'Yes sir, we do have milk for sale. I told Martha it would sell. She figured everyone who wanted milk had a cow. Told her we're getting too big for that. We got a town ice house where we cut two-foot-thick ice from the pond in the winter and pack it down with layers of straw. With the straw the ice will last most years until August. Got me this ice chest I put the milk in.'

Wade took a quart and went outside town to camp for the night. He cooked up some of the oatmeal and used the milk on it. He drank the rest. It had been weeks since he'd had any milk. As usual he moved away from his dying fire when he rolled out his blanket.

* * *

The next morning he rode as soon as the sun came up. In the small town of Milepost, eight miles up the road, he talked to the town marshal.

'Oh, yeah, One Hand was here. I met him as soon as he came into town. I had two deputies with me and we all had double barreled Greeners. We ushered him right out on the north road and watched him for two miles to be sure he kept moving.'

Wade had a quick sandwich at a café and two glasses of milk, then rode north. He was less than four hours behind One Hand. That made him think through what he had to do when he found him. First he had to be sure he was the man who shot his pa. What if he wouldn't admit it?

He would have to surprise One Hand somehow. Shoot him in the back? Probably not. Why not? He hadn't given Pa no chance. One Hand didn't deserve a chance.

Wade kept thinking about it as he rode. A sign at the edge of Milepost pointed north toward the next town of Grassland. The marker said it was fourteen miles. Maybe the Rebel would slow down and stay all night there. If so, Wade should be able to catch him in that town. He unsnapped the flap on his saddle as he rode and took out his hoard of money. Only thirty dollars left. He fished out a ten-dollar bill and put the rest away. He should be able to buy a used Greener shotgun for ten dollars. Could he walk around a town carrying a shotgun? Not likely. First he'd have to find the man, then make sure he was the Rebel raider. Then he'd figure out how he was going to kill him.

* * *

Four hours later the first thing he saw when he came into Grassland was a Wanted poster nailed to an oak tree at the edge of town. It was the One Hand poster offering a $200 reward. He checked with the town marshal who said there were no reports that the wanted man had been in town. Wade went to the general store and bought the only Greener the man had, a single-shot. He took it and a box of a dozen buckshot shells and had change from his ten-dollar bill.

What would the outlaw do? He knew now that there was a Wanted poster on him. He must have seen it and detoured around the town. If so he must still be heading north toward Topeka. Wade pushed the Greener into a sling he had fashioned from some rope. The sling tied to the saddle kept the Greener handy and safe from falling out. He rode north. It would be dark in an hour. Chances were that One Hand would find a spot to camp for the night. If he lit a fire, Wade would be able to find him.

Would he sleep beside it? It was brisk at night but not cold. He wondered how trail-wise One Hand really was?

Less than a half-hour out of Grassland, Wade smelled wood smoke. Smoke in a town means nothing and people never notice it. But out in the open, where usually there is no smoke, a wood fire's scent can carry for miles on a gentle breeze. If the wind is coming from the fire, it can be a beacon to lead an inquisitive man straight to the blaze. It was almost dark.

Wade rode ahead slowly. Fifteen minutes later it was fully dark and he could see the glow of a fire ahead. One Hand could still be cooking his supper. Too early for him to bed down. Wade eased his mount forward. There was no moonlight that night. It was dark-on blackness except fifty yards ahead at the fire. It was too big to be a cooking fire. So supper was over. The blaze was in a small grove of rusty blackhaw trees beside a creek. Wade walked his mount within forty yards of the fire and looked around it carefully. Nobody there.

He checked again. So the gunman had moved away and was sleeping. Wade saw a horse at the far side of the firelight. He rode that way, screened by the blackhaw and brush, caught the groundtied mount's reins and led the bare-backed horse away. He went thirty yards and tied both horses to a small alder. There had been no horse-talk between the two animals. Both must be too tired to snort at each other.

Wade took the Greener and six shells. He slid one shell into the chamber on the shotgun and closed the barrel quietly, then moved cautiously toward the fire. Still no one there. He began to circle the fire twenty yards out. Wade moved as he had as a boy hunting wild turkeys in Missouri: one small step at a time, making sure he didn't break a dry stick or rustle any leaves. He eased through the woods like a black shadow. He was halfway around the circle on the far side of the four-foot-wide creek when he heard a snore.

Wade grinned. He turned and crept that direction. It took him five minutes of slow and slower movement to find the shootist. He lay with his head on his saddle and a sheepskin coat thrown over him. His right hand was on top of the coat holding a six-gun.

Get the gun.

Wade moved again, snail slow, working up from behind the saddle. When he could touch it, he stood, then took two quick steps. With the second one he rammed his boot down on One Hand's right wrist jolting the six-gun out of his hand and bringing a roar of anger and rage. Wade grabbed the killer's six-gun and jumped back out of reach.

'What's happening? Who are you?' One Hand bellowed.

'I'm your worst nightmare, Larch,'

Wade said from eight feet away.

'What? Who are you? Give me back my weapon.'

'Not a chance. My name is Wade Tretter, but you wouldn't remember the name. I bring you greetings from the Captain and Rudy.'

'What? The Captain and Rudy? How do you know them?'

'I know it all. Since you recognize the names, you were one of four Rebel raiders who hit our farm in Missouri four years ago. Small place. The man came out of the house and offered to shoe your mounts. You four shot him down without a word.'

'Don't know what you're talking about. Look, you want money, I can give you money.'

'I don't want your money.'

'Let me stand up and look at you.'

'No, stay where you are.' Wade pulled the hammer on the killer's six-gun to full cock. One Hand pushed the sheepskin coat off his legs and started to move. Wade put a shot into the sheepskin six inches from his right leg.

'Hey, you a rawhider?'

'Wrong. The next one goes in your kneecap.' Wade watched the gunman who must be judging his chances. He glared at Wade in the dim light.

'I need some answers. Who was the raider with the full beard with you? The one who stole the Greener and a rifle from the cabin?'

'Don't know what you're talking about . . . ' One Hand lunged for his left leg, had a hideout revolver out of leather and lifted it.

Wade fired again, hitting the outlaw in the right shoulder, spinning the small gun out of sight.

'Easy, wild man. We can work this out.'

'At least I gave you a chance. Not like you did when you shot down my pa.'

'He was just a small time rancher.'

'What was the brown-bearded man's name?'

'I'm bleeding to death. Shot me, you sidewinder.'

'The name of the bearded one, or I'll put a round in your left leg.'

Wade moved closer in the dim light and aimed the weapon.

'All right, all right. The beard was Bert Daniels.'

'What's Rudy's last name?'

'No talk, I'm bleeding to death.' He paused. Wade cocked the six-gun. 'All right, he's Rudy Anderson and the Captain is John Brewer. Now get me back into town to a doctor.'

'Why aren't you with the others?'

'The yellow-bellies robbed me of my money and my guns and dumped me in a little town in Missouri. Said I was too easy to identify. Low life. I'd gun them down in a second if I could find them.'

'Where are the three men now?'

'Headed west somewhere. I don't know.'

'How about the Flying W Ranch?'

'How'd you know about that?'

'I was in the weeds out by the creek watching you four raiders kill my parents. I made myself a promise then.'

'Look, I didn't hurt your ma. Dumb Daniels did that. You can't blame me for your pa. I think I missed him when I shot.'

'You didn't. I found four bullet holes in his chest.'

'So what happens now? You ain't the kind of a young kid who shoots a man down in cold blood.'

'True, but my blood's been getting hotter and hotter for almost four years now, Larch. I'd say your One Hand days are over.'

Before Wade knew it the man reared up and surged forward, jolting toward Wade, his arms flailing at the six-gun. Wade shot him three times in the chest and he fell at Wade's feet.

One Hand looked up.

'Good you did it. Now I don't have to wait for some galoot to prove he's faster than me. I been waiting.' He coughed up blood and spit it out. 'No more waiting.' He gave one last sigh and his head slumped. Wade stared down at the gunman. He wondered whether he would cry, but his eyes were dry. He'd just killed a man. He gasped and turned away as his stomach boiled. A moment later he leaned against a tree and vomited. His lunch came up and then dry heaves. He sagged to his knees and wiped off his mouth. He left Larch where he lay and went back to the creek. There he washed out his mouth and had a long drink.

Dead. One of the killers was dead. He had been trying to figure out what to do when One Hand surged forward. He wondered whether he could have executed the man. Shot him down counting on all of his anger and hatred. He didn't have to figure it out. What would he do when he found the next Rebel raider? Could he level his six-gun and blow the man straight into Hades? He simply didn't know. He moved to the fire. After he warmed himself, he put out the flames, then went to his horse, and took off the saddle. He found a spot by the creek and rolled out his blanket up wind from where the fire had been. Then he tried to go to sleep.

He couldn't drop off. He kept reliving the shoot-out with One Hand. After he'd been over it, a hundred times it seemed, the whole scene faded and he drifted into a dream-troubled sleep.

* * *

The next morning he checked through One Hand's saddle-bags and his carpetbag of belongings. The man had stolen from his family. This was paying back the Tretter family. He found over $300 in gold and paper money. He took that and the .44 and two boxes of shells. Wade tossed the saddle on to One Hand's mount and strapped it down. Then he heaved One Hand's body across the killer's own saddled horse and tied him on. It was a slow ride into Grassland. The town marshal looked at the body draped over the horse.

'Yep, that sure enough looks like the man on the poster. You can't collect the reward here. We got no telegraph and the mail is slow going south. You got some riding to do.'

Wade had wondered how he would collect. He figured he might as well get the reward money. It took him all the rest of the day to ride to Johnson Creek. He stopped at the sheriff's office and went inside.

An hour later he had the $200, the sheriff had his killer, and Wade rode out of town west. After five miles he stopped in some shade, hid part of the money in his secret spot on his saddle, the rest of it and the gold coins in his cooking gear, and kept on riding. Now he had some more cash for an emergency. He wondered how far it was to the Flying W cattle ranch?

6

Western Kansas
14 May 1869

It took Wade Tretter almost another year to work his way into the western part of Kansas. He'd chased down three seemingly good leads on two of the Rebel raiders, only to find men with the same name but who were not the killers he sought.

He was eighteen now, nearing his full growth at six feet one inch tall and a well-toned body of 180 pounds.

He could shoot his six-gun much better now. For a month he'd stayed in a little cowtown where there was plenty of farrier business. An old gunhand named Oliver, in his sixties, took a fancy to Wade and soon Wade confided to Oliver about the tragedy of his family and his quest. Oliver had been a fast draw ten years ago. Three drunken cowhands had called him out — him against all three. He put down two of them before the third man's round hit his gun hand. That was the end of his shooting career. He had settled down on a little cattle ranch.

Oliver made Wade his pupil and trained him every day how to draw, aim, and shoot his six-gun. At the end of the month he could outdraw Oliver in their dry-run practice.

'You're good, Wade,' Oliver said. 'Just make sure you get off an accurate shot. Don't worry about outdrawing the other man. Your one job is to shoot straight and true. Remember, most gunfights never last long enough for a second shot.'

They worked together for two hours every day on shooting from the hip right after drawing.

When he came to Flint, Kansas, Wade read the painted sign at the edge of town. 'Population 2,464.' The last number four had been painted out and a crudely drawn figure five replaced it. This was the biggest town he'd seen for a month. He rented a hotel room for the night for a dollar and spent another quarter for three buckets of hot water brought to the bathroom. After soaking and scrubbing and soaking again, he felt clean and ready for a big noon meal.

At every café he looked for a girl like Alice, but there was never one. He had the special of the day, roast beef, vegetables, fresh-baked dinner rolls, and a baked potato and brown gravy. He had learned to drink coffee last winter mostly to keep warm.

That afternoon he met with the county sheriff. Now that he knew the killers' names it made things easier. The sheriff wore a six-gun while sitting at his desk. He was a large man, solid, but with a paunch hanging over his belt. He was over fifty and probably never went out of the office.

'Sheriff, I'm Wade Tretter. I'm hunting three men.'

The sheriff stood and held out his hand. 'Name's Wilson. Been sheriff here for eight years. Who you hunting?'

'Trying to track down Bert Daniels, John Brewer, and Rudy Anderson.'

The sheriff sighed. 'We get one or two men a week in here looking for somebody. Usually they're angry and impatient. Something to do with the war?'

'Afraid so.'

'Enough said. One of them names sounds familiar. Let me check some back files. Last year sometime.' He went to a shelf and took down a box. The sheriff sorted through it for ten minutes, grunted and pulled out an envelope with a name on the top.

'That name was Bert J. Daniels?'

'Didn't know about the J. Did he have a crippled left arm?'

'Yep. Got to be the same guy. Shows here he was thirty-six years old last year, brown hair, and a brown beard. Jailed him for drunk and disorderly. Next day we let him out and he cut up a dance hall girl. It wasn't bad and she didn't press charges, so I had to let him go. He'd been in town a month. Claimed he was a cowboy but he didn't have the rope burns on his hands. He wasn't a gambler. I don't know what he did.'

The sheriff handed the folder to Wade who read the rest of it. He listed Flint, Colorado as his home town.

'He still around?'

'Don't remember seeing him. Talk to them at the Last Chance saloon. That was where he used to hang out.'

Wade thanked the sheriff who frowned.

'Mr Tretter, just curious. You mean to do some harm to this man?'

'I might.'

'What did he do to you? Just curious.'

'He killed my father and mother in Missouri four years ago just before the war ended. He was a Rebel raider.'

'You have a Wanted poster on him?'

'Ain't none. My word against his.'

Sheriff Wilson sat down and scowled.

‘A Kansas jury would never convict him on your lone testimony. Maybe in Missouri.’ He stared hard at Wade. ‘You do him harm, Mr Tretter, and I’d have to arrest you.’

Wade watched the steely eyes of the lawman. ‘I figured that, Sheriff. But if he gets hurt, it’ll be in a fair fight. Self-defense.’ He turned, walked out of the office and headed for the Last Chance Saloon.

Behind the bar a thick-set man with no neck and small eyes stared at Wade. Wade went to the bar, ordered a beer, paid a dime for it, then sipped it as he looked around. A year ago Daniels had a brown beard, the sheriff had said. None of the men he could see had a beard. Only two men stood at the bar and neither had face hair. He turned back to the bartender.

Wade motioned him down the bar. The man moved slowly, a frown building on his square-cut face.

‘Heard that Bert Daniels would be here today.’

'How could you hear that? You're new in town.'

Wade nodded. 'Yeah, new. Still looking for Daniels. He been in today or last night?'

'Comes in now and then. He's punching cows most of the time.'

'What ranch does he ride for?'

'Don't rightly know why I should tell you. You're a stranger, might be a lawman. Besides, he's a friend of mine.'

Wade sipped at his beer, then put down the mug and frowned at the bar keep. 'Look, I'm not a lawman. I don't have a Wanted poster for Bert. I just need to find him and talk to him.'

The man behind the bar polished the mahogany that didn't need it. He hooded his eyes, then looked at Wade.

'Just talk?'

'I just need some information.'

The barkeep wiped a glass and stared hard at Wade. 'OK, but if he gets hurt, I'm coming after you. He works for the Lazy L about five miles out on the west road, right along the Waverly River. Has a big gatepost over the lane into the place.'

Wade nodded. 'Thanks.' He finished the beer and left the saloon. Had he just told a huge lie? He had to find out whether he knew where the other two Rebel raiders were. Before or after he found out there could be some gun action. He would wait and see how Bert Daniels played it. Wade untied Betsy, mounted, and walked her out the west road along the Waverly River.

He covered the five miles in a little under an hour and a half. It was afternoon by the time he found the big posts and a gate at the Lazy L ranch. He rode down the lane a quarter of a mile to the ranch buildings, which appeared to be a good-sized spread. Three men were at the corral as he rode up. Two nodded, the third came off the top rail where he had been watching a cowboy breaking a horse. The man held up his hand to Wade, who was still mounted.

'Afternoon, I'm George Langdon.

This is my Lazy L. Looking for work?'

'Wade Tretter, Mr Langdon. No sir. I'm trying to find a friend of mine, Bert Daniels. He work for you?'

Caution tinged the rancher's face. He stepped back a pace and nodded. ''Deed he does. He's the one on the nag out there in the corral. He's great with horses.'

'Mind if I wait until he's through and then talk with him?'

'Sure he's a friend?'

'He probably won't remember me but we've met before.'

Another small lie. He stepped off Betsy and tied her to the corral rail, then watched the cowboy riding the partly broken quarter horse. She went along easy for a while, then bucked, twisted, snorted, and raced for the fence. At the last moment she spun away. Three times more the horse did much the same thing. Daniels talked to the mount all the time, soft and gentle. At last she walked sedately three times around the corral. Daniels brought her over and stepped out of the saddle. He kept talking to the bay as he unfastened the cinch strap and lifted the saddle off her. She stepped around for a moment, then calmed. He took the bridle off and left her standing there. She turned her long neck, looked at Daniels, then walked away.

'Good work, Daniels,' Langdon said.

Daniels nodded.

Wade could see that he still had a brown beard; now it was trimmed short and the moustache was full. Daniels climbed to the top rail and dropped out of the corral. Langdon waved him over and they spoke. Both looked at Wade.

Daniels built a stern frown as he walked toward Wade. The man looked his thirty-six or -seven years. His hands showed the rope burns of a working cowboy. The lie came easier this time.

'Mr Daniels,' Wade said holding out his hand. 'You probably don't remember me, Wade Tretter. From Columbus back in Ohio.'

Daniels scowled and shook his head.

'Right. Never met you.'

'Yes, we probably never did meet, or if we did I was just a small boy. My ma said if I ever got to Kansas to see if I could find Mr Bert J. Daniels. Daniels was her maiden name and Bert was one of her nephews. Heard there was a Bert Daniels out here, so thought I'd take a chance that you might have kin back in Ohio.'

'That ain't me. Never heard of Columbus. I'm from Tennessee.'

'Well, don't that beat all. Figured I might get lucky and find some kin out here. So, I better be moving back to town. You did good on that mustang out there. That a wild one you caught?'

'Nope. We raised her. She just ain't never been saddled before.' He turned and walked away and Wade saw that Bert never straightened out his left arm. It went out three quarters of the way and stopped. His left hand hung six inches higher than his right.

Wade tried to remember that fateful day four years ago. What had the man with the brown beard and brown hair looked like? He had no idea. He walked over to Betsy, mounted, waved at the ranch owner, then rode down the lane toward town.

He had been ninety per cent sure that Daniels was the man he hunted. The gimpy arm was the clincher. Wade knew that he needed a plan to get the man alone. He could go back after dark and roust him from the bunkhouse, riding him out into the plains and grill him until he got some satisfaction as to where the other two men were. That involved a huge risk.

He could wait until tomorrow, hoping Daniels would ride out on the range on some project. But would it happen, and then, would he be alone?

* * *

Usually he didn't pay much attention to what day of the week it was, but when he had supper in the café, he observed a notice on the menu. It said: Good

Morning! This is Saturday, and we hope that you fare well.

Saturday. Saturday night was the traditional time for cowboys to head for town, get drunk and blow off steam after a tough week on the range. Would Bert Daniels be coming to town tonight? In two hours he should know. His pocket watch showed him that it was about 5.30. The range hands would eat at five and be saddled up and heading for town by six. It would still be light by then. Sunset wasn't until about seven o'clock these summer days. He could find a place out of sight near the trail and wait and see if Bert Daniels rode into town.

Wade found a spot two miles from town. The river ran close to the trail here and he pushed into some heavy growth of brush and pawpaw, elder and deerberry trees. He dismounted, let Betsy drink, and then settled down to wait. He carved out a viewing port in some brush and weeds so he could see up-trail half a mile, yet nobody could spot him. His lair was about twenty feet from the trail.

He pulled some beef jerky from his food pack and chewed on it. Wade waited an hour and then he saw a faint trail of dust where some horses headed down the dirt road toward him. How many? One would be perfect if it were Daniels. Two would work, but he'd have to follow them into town and get Daniels alone. Most likely the cowboys were heading for some saloon.

Ten minutes later he watched the three riders go past him at a walk. They laughed and told jokes and some story about a wild stallion. Then they were gone. He let them have a half-mile start, then followed. When they came to the edge of town he hurried so he could watch where they went. They passed the first saloon and tied their horses at the second watering hole.

He tied Betsy near their horses, went inside, got a beer at the bar, and sat at a far table where no one played poker. The three Lazy L riders had two beers each and sat at a table across the room. Wade kept his gray Stetson pulled low on his face so Daniels wouldn't recognize him.

As he watched, one of them went to the back door, where there would be an outhouse. The other one went to the bar for more beer. Daniels was left sitting at the table working on his second beer.

Wade thought of taking Daniels while he was alone at the table. That meant he'd have to get him out the front door without him screaming for help. No. Wait. The other two came back. They watched a poker game for a while. Then Daniels said something that made the other two laugh and headed for the back door and maybe to the outhouse.

This was his chance. Wade came to his feet and followed. He eased the back door open and looked out. The small shack sat to the left and had the door closed. Wade slipped out and waited just outside the outhouse. When the door opened, he rammed his six-gun's muzzle in Daniel's back.

'What the — '

'Don't talk, Daniels, just walk down the alley.'

'Your voice. You're the guy who was out at the ranch. I told you I ain't any of your kin.'

'I thank God for that.' Wade waved his iron at him. 'I'll take your weapon, you won't need it. Keep walking toward the end of the alley. We'll go around front and get the horses.'

'My buddies will miss me.'

'They probably think you're still in the outhouse. Move.'

They walked to the end of the alley and then to the front of the saloon where the horses stood.

'We're going to ride out of town where we can have a nice quiet talk.'

'You're crazy. I told you you're none of my kin.'

'I know that, Daniels. You ever hear of a gent by the name of Captain John Brewer?'

Daniels' head snapped up and his

eyes squinted. 'Captain John? How do you know his name? Just who are you, kid?'

'Don't worry about it. Just mount up, cowboy, and ride.'

They walked their horses three blocks to the edge of town, then rode west into the prairie. They passed a house on the edge of a small farm, then went off the road and into a stand of black oak a half-mile farther on.

'Get down,' Wade said.

When both of them were on the ground Wade waved the cowboy to a cleared spot. 'Now, Daniels, you and me gonna have us one good old talk. Where can I find Captain Brewer, and his buddy, Rudy Anderson?'

'Anderson, too?' Daniels said. 'You must have known us that last few days of the war. Four of us split off from the company and went out on our own.' He shook his head. 'I don't believe it. You mean you're somebody from one of those families . . . ' His voice faded and he shivered. Then he pointed his finger at the ground just behind Wade.

'Hey, quiet, don't move, not a muscle. There's a big rattler coiled up not a foot from your boots. He's about ready to strike. Hold absolutely still. You move a whisker and he'll strike two or three times before you can move. Stay still and I can club him with a stick.'

Wade frowned. He didn't know whether there were rattlesnakes in this part of Kansas or not. For just a fraction of a second he turned his head and looked behind. In an instant he knew it was a mistake. By the time he had lifted the six-gun to aim it at where Daniels had been, the cowboy had slammed into Wade's chest with his shoulder. It jolted him backwards and knocked the gun out of his hand. They both stumbled and fell. Wade's chest hurt. He hit the ground hard and felt Daniels on top of him for just a moment. The cowboy rolled away, leaped to his feet and sprinted ten yards to his horse. He jumped on board over the back quarters, hit his heels into the nag's flanks and raced out of the woods.

Wade cursed himself as he sat up, hurried to his feet and searched in the darkness for his six-gun. He found it and shoved it into his holster. He still had Daniels's gun pushed into his belt. He ran for his horse and stepped into the saddle. For a moment he was quiet, listening to the sound of the hoofs. They were soft and heading across country through an open field. Wade kicked Betsy in the flanks and galloped after the Rebel raider. He wasn't going to let him get away.

7

Wade rode hard for five minutes, then stopped, and listened. He could hear the other horse ahead of him. The clouds played tag with the moon offering ten-minute chunks of bright moonlight from an almost full moon. Wade rode harder. He could see the other rider now and then and, as he judged the direction he figured that Daniels was circling around and heading back to the Lazy L.

Wade turned to the right in what would be a short cut across the arc and bring him into the area just west of the Lazy L ranch a half-mile before Daniels could get there. It was a gamble. If Daniels changed direction and kept going due west, he would be lost out in the rangeland.

Wade let Betsy rest for a quarter-mile of walking, then rode her at a gallop for a mile before he reined in for another resting walk. He had to be right. Daniels would try for his home base. He was one of the owner's favorites. If Daniels got back to the ranch, there was no way that Wade could dig him out.

He rode hard again, saw the lights of the ranch house ahead, and angled more to the west. When he was a half-mile out he found a thicket of hazel alder, worked his way into it, then turned and watched to the west. He wished that he had a rope. Then he could lasso Daniels, pull him off his mount and drag him until he was ready to talk.

Ten minutes later he heard a horse coming from the west. It was cantering. It was a pace that most horses came to naturally.

The clouds co-operated and broke for the moon to shine through. He saw the rider coming now, but he was too far away to be sure who it was. Who else would be coming to the ranch from this direction? He would wait until the rider was twenty yards away, then burst out of the cover at a gallop, and be on top of him before he could react. If the rider wasn't Daniels, he'd apologize and ride on.

He could send a warning shot over the rider's head but that might alert someone from the ranch.

The rider came closer and, at the right moment Wade dug his heels into Betsy. She charged out of the brush directly into the path of the other horseman. Daniels had time only to pull back on the reins. The horse reared. Daniels wasn't ready for it and was bucked off the horse. He hit the ground hard.

Wade rode up and leveled his six-gun at him.

'Daniels, don't move. Just sit there in the dirt. I want some answers and I want them right now. Move an inch and you're dead meat. You understand?'

'You polecat. I ain't telling you a thing.'

Wade slid down on the off side of

Betsy, careful to keep his Colt trained on Daniels. He was in the dirt, half-lying down. Wade checked the area around them. There *were* rattlesnakes in Kansas, he remembered now. The snakes gave him an idea.

'OK, Daniels. Where is Rudy Anderson?'

'Don't know.'

'You do know. You're betting your life that you know. If you don't you're no more use to me alive than dead. I remember you running out of the house in Missouri with my ma's blood on your hunting knife. You killed my mother. I should kill you right now.'

'How you know that?'

'I was out by the creek watching. My pa warned us about guys like you coming in. I hid close by and heard it all, saw it, and heard my ma scream when you killed her. Now, I'm asking you one more time. Where can I find Rudy Anderson and Captain John Brewer?'

'Hey, I ain't their mother.'

Wade felt his anger rising. He wanted to shoot the killer right then. Blast him off the planet and into Hades. His anger surged and peaked as he moved his six-gun and shot Daniels in his right knee. The sound of the gunshot came sharp and clear. He hoped everyone at the ranch more than a half-mile away was sound asleep.

Daniels screamed in agony. He keened and bellowed in rage: 'You shot me! You idiot. I'm bleeding to death.'

'Every time you give me the wrong answer, I'll shoot you again. You've got two arms, two shoulders and another leg. Now, once more: where can I find your two killing partners?'

Daniels shook his head. He wasn't saying a thing. Then he couldn't give the wrong answer. Wade hesitated. He didn't want to risk another shot.

'Daniels, you know that these warm nights the copperhead rattler comes out to feed? True. Bet I could kick up one around here if I worked at it. Old Indian trick about tying a man down flat on his belly with arms and legs stretched out and tied down to stakes. Then tie a rattler within reach of the man's head. All you have to do to keep from being struck by the snake is to hold your head up. 'Course pretty soon your neck gets tired and your head comes down a little at a time. The old rattler has tried to strike twice before. Now he spots the target within range and he gets you in the side of the face. Goodbye Daniels.'

The cowboy killer didn't respond.

'So, Daniels. Do I kick up a copperhead to play the game with, or do you want to tell me where your two murdering buddies are?'

Daniels bellowed in anger and rage. His voice turned into a moan and he glared at Wade. He tried to stop the flow of blood from his knee. He'd tied his kerchief around it, but still blood stained through it and dripped into the dry ground. His scream came again, a cry of fury and frustration, as he writhed on the ground, holding his knee.

'Oh, I bring you greetings from another friend of yours, Larch Creighton. You remember him, the guy with only one hand. I found him over in Grassland. Sends his regards. He was really furious that you robbed him and kicked him out of your group. He's not worried about it now. He's planted six feet under back in Johnson Creek. No wonder you haven't heard from him.'

'You're a madman. I never even met your ma. You've got the wrong man. Lots of guys named Daniels around.'

Wade felt his fury rising again. How could he deny it? How could this murdering filthy excuse for a human being do that? He sighted in and shot Daniels in the other leg high in his thigh. Daniels screamed into the dark night. His voice wavered, then fell, and he yelled out a string of profanities. His voice became a wild screech that echoed through the dark Kansas plains.

'Hey, you hands at the Lazy L. Come help me. This crazy man is shooting me.'

'Afraid it's a little bit far away for them to hear you. Guess I'm going to have to kick up a copperhead after all. I better get you tied down to some stakes first. Roll over on your belly, cow-puncher. Get your lying face in the dirt and rocks.'

'No.'

'Wrong answer again, Daniels. I think I'll do your right shoulder this time.' He lifted the six-gun and cocked the hammer.

'Hold it,' Daniels bellowed just after Wade cocked the Colt.

'Second thoughts?'

'Look, I've got two thousand in gold coins nobody knows about. That's why the guys hated me. I wouldn't tell them if I had it or if I lost it. I hid it in my saddle under an extra flap of leather. Let me get my saddle and I'll show you. All two thousand in gold is yours.'

'Nice try, Daniels. If you had that money they would have found it. Then they would have dumped you out in nowhere. I'm rattlesnake hunting.'

'No, no. I hate snakes.' Daniels looked around where he sat and edged over into a more open space. 'OK. Last I heard them talking, they were heading for the Flying W. That's near East Bend. A Kansas town. Anderson has some friends there.'

'East Bend. Where is that?'

'About twenty miles from the Colorado and the Nebraska borders. Little town of four thousand. North and west of here about fifty miles.'

'Why didn't you go with them?'

'They ditched me. Said I was a country man and they were city folks. Didn't want me to dirty them up. Cowboy work more to my way of living.'

'Why did you kill my ma back in Missouri?'

'She called me filthy names. No woman ever called me names like that.'

'What did you expect? You were robbing her. You'd just killed her husband.'

'No sir. I didn't hurt her.'

'I saw your bloody knife. Heard what the guys said to you.'

'She made me mad. So mad I couldn't think straight.'

'That's how mad I am right now, Daniels. That mean I can knife you to death just because you're making me furious?' He reached to his holster and took out the four-inch knife with a gleaming blade.

Daniels scooted back a foot. 'No. No, sir. You don't look wild and mad to me.'

'You sorry you killed my ma and pa?'

'Sorry? Sure. I was young and wild. The war was on. We was a special Rebel unit for the Confederacy.'

'Not true. You were murdering freebooters. You raided north and south alike burning and murdering. You never left witnesses.'

Wade wanted to be angry, to be furious, and to be so outraged that he could put a bullet right between the killer's eyes. He wasn't sure he could do it. The burning anger he had felt before never came back. That scared him a little. He was calm, collected, thinking fast but thinking straight. He thought of his wonderful mother, how she had schooled him in reading and writing. He thought of his honest, hard-working pa. He lived right from wrong every day.

Could he draw down on this vermin, this murderer who might have snuffed out the lives of ten or twenty human beings? He had to do it. That frightened him a little. He was sure he could kill this vermin. It was nothing more serious than squashing a bug in the dirt, or shooting a rabbit for supper.

He cocked the six-gun and did what the old man in Missouri told him to do, pointed his finger at the killer's face and squeezed the trigger. The blasting sound of the .44-caliber round going off in the total quiet of the dark plains of Kansas startled Wade. He looked with surprise as the bullet slammed into Bert Daniels' forehead, rammed through his brain and exploded out the back of his head taking half of his skull with the heavy slug. Daniels' head flopped backward and then the rest of his body slammed into the solid Kansas prairie.

'Oh, my God,' Wade said. He blinked back tears. He stood looking at the corpse of the second of the four Rebel raiders who had killed his parents. To his surprise he said a little prayer his mother had taught him at a funeral.

'May the Lord have mercy on your soul. You may not have been a perfect human being but you were one of God's creatures. May you rest in peace.'

8

Wade mounted and looked around for Daniels' horse. He found her grazing a short distance away. He brought her back and hoisted Daniels' corpse over the saddle belly down, then tied his hands and feet together under the horse's stomach. He rode leading the mount until he was within 300 yards of the Lazy L ranch buildings. There he gave the horse her head and she walked toward her home corral.

Wade turned and rode, angling north and to the west. He wasn't sure how far this new town was but Daniels had said it was about fifty miles. That could mean anywhere from twenty to a hundred. He would ride all night. It was still early. He wanted to be out of the county before daylight. There was a chance that the sheriff might come looking for him as soon as Daniels' death was reported.

He rode until midnight. He could tell time by the North Star and how far the big dipper had rotated around it. Cowboys called it star time. By ten o'clock the two bottom pointer stars of the cup of the dipper were level east and west and pointing at the North Star. By midnight the pointer stars on the cup had rotated down to the four o'clock position, pointing upward.

It was nearly midnight by star time when he found a trail heading north. He took it and the going was easier. He walked Betsy. She could make four miles an hour with no strain and keep it up for ten hours. Even thirty-two miles should put him well out of reach of the local sheriff.

Wade took a break about two o'clock. He figured he'd covered over fifteen miles. He gave Betsy a drink at a stream and stretched out under a big silver maple. He dozed off for a moment then stood and walked around. He couldn't afford to go to sleep this close to the Lazy L ranch.

Twenty minutes later he rode again. By seven o'clock he was so tired he could hardly sit his saddle. He found a small creek with some thick brush, a stand of river willow, and worked into it far enough to hide Betsy and himself. He tied Betsy to a willow and lay down on the grass. He slept before he knew it.

When he awoke at two o'clock that afternoon the first thing he did was check his back trail. He couldn't see anyone following him. Good. He looked in his food sack. Getting low. He had an apple and a can of pears and some beef jerky for his meal, then cinched up the saddle and rode again.

The second day away from Daniels' home ranch, he came to a settlement. A sign at the edge of the place called it Warren, Kansas.

So he was still in Kansas and hadn't blundered into Nebraska. He had supper at a small restaurant. It only had a counter, no tables, and one woman seemed to be cook and waitress.

The waitress was about thirty, he guessed, medium height for a woman and on the chunky side. He had the only item on the supper menu: beef stew, with big chunks of meat, potatoes, carrots, parsnips, cabbage, green beans, and onions mixed into it in a gut-filling meal. He also had thick slices of bread, strawberry jam and two cups of coffee. When he was done she brought him a piece of pie.

'My name is June. I own this place. During the day I have a girl who helps, but I don't get much supper trade. Only four hundred folks live in town, and most don't have much money to eat out. But I manage. You just passing through?'

'Yes, ma'am. Looking for farrier work as well.'

'Don't know nothing about that. Enjoy your pie. Time for me to close up.'

* * *

He took a room at the town's only hotel that offered him a choice of its four rooms for seventy-five cents a night. He had breakfast the next morning at June's café. He asked her if she'd ever heard of the town of East Bend.

'Yeah, heard of it. Never been there. On up north somewhere. I think it's still in Kansas, but it might be across the state line into Nebraska.'

'Any idea how far?'

'Not a guess.'

'Well, I got to be moving on. I got me some important business up north. But, if I come back this way, I'll be sure to stop by for supper.'

June laughed. 'Yeah, I've heard that before.'

Ten minutes later he was saddled up and getting traveling supplies at the general store. He picked out a stock of food and paid for it from some of the money from his saddle bank. He only had twenty dollars left from the original cattle sale back in Missouri. Under that lay the $200 from the Wanted poster on

Larch. The other money from Larch was in his tool case.

The merchant who ran the mercantile was about fifty, Wade figured. He was almost bald with fringes of graying hair round the sides and in back, and a pair of spectacles perched on the end of his nose.

'East Bend. Yep, I've heard of it. Had a sister up that way somewhere. I'd say you need to go north and then west some toward the Colorado state line. We're up here in the corner of Kansas.'

Outside Wade packed his food bag in back of his saddle along with his camping gear and his farrier kit. Then he rode. A semblance of a trail led north. It wasn't even a wagon road and it tended to fade away and then get stronger as it neared cattle spreads.

By noon he figured he'd covered ten miles. He looked around and realized that he couldn't see another human being or any signs that there ever had been anyone here. No cattle, no horses, no fences, not a building anywhere. Just the unending prairie, the gently swaying grass, and a host of prairie dogs popping out of their holes to watch him ride past.

It was another three hours before he spotted smoke on the horizon. He had no idea how far away it was, but smoke meant men, and probably a small town, maybe East Bend itself. Or it could be Indians.

By five o'clock he seemed to be just as far from the smoke as when he'd first seen it. He decided to make camp and cook himself up a good supper. Maybe some bacon, then in the bacon grease he'd fry some sliced potatoes and onions. He'd cook some of the fresh peas he'd bought at the last store. Just thinking about it made him hungry.

* * *

About ten o'clock the next morning he came to some ranch buildings. He rode along a short lane and called to a cowboy he saw riding in from the other direction.

'Morning,' Wade said.

'Hi, stranger.'

'Looks like I'm lost. I'm hunting East Bend. You any idea where it is?'

The cowboy chuckled. 'Yeah, you ain't lost. That's it just about three miles down the road. Can't miss it. Don't know why you want to go there. Funny little town. Not much to it. I can't figure out why folks want to live there. I was wondering maybe you was looking for a riding job. We got a couple of vacant beds in the bunkhouse and we'll be doing a round-up before long.'

'Thanks for the offer, but I'm not much of a cowhand. I do need to get into that town. Much obliged for your help.' He waved and rode out along the lane to the wagon road, then headed for East Bend at a little faster clip. As he rode toward the town he yearned for a big juicy steak.

As he came up to it, he realized that the town of East Bend looked pretty good. He later learned it was about ten miles east of the Colorado border and the same distance away from the Nebraska state line to the north. He had intended to camp outside of town and look it over carefully first, but by the time he rode close it was near noon. He went right in, tied up at a rail outside the first café he saw, and headed toward it for that steak. He stopped at the horse-watering trough to wash off his hands and face and dried them with the kerchief from around his neck. He looked up the street. A town of about 2,000, not 4,000 like somebody had told him. Big enough to support a farrier.

He stepped into the café, went to the counter, and ordered his meal. The steak, baked potato, vegetables, two pieces of pie and two cups of good coffee filled him. The waitress watched him eating and stopped by his table.

'More pie? More coffee? Looks like you been on the trail for a time.'

'You're right. Best meal I've had in

two weeks.' She had told him her name was Beulah and she'd lived in East Bend most of her life.

'Passing through or staying?' she asked. 'Yeah, I know. Folks say I'm nosy. But how you gonna find out anything if you don't ask?'

'Figured I might stay a while, Beulah. This a good town?'

'Good as any. From looks of your hands, you don't have no rope burns, so you can't be a cowboy.'

'I'm a farrier. Hope you don't have one in town.'

'Nope. We don't. Old Gus down at the blacksmith's does that work, but he hates it. Got himself kicked again last week. Not too good a hand getting the nails set right, somebody told me.'

'That will do it.' He thanked her, paid his bill, sixty cents. The dime extra was for the second piece of pie, Beulah told him. Outside he stretched. He'd been in the saddle too long. There were two hotels. One three stories and the other two. The one with three levels had recently been painted, the boardwalk in front of it was well-made, and level. It was probably more expensive too, he decided. So? He had over four dollars left from his last farrier work. He walked Betsy over to the better hotel, tied her to the rail, and went inside.

A half-hour later he had moved everything he owned except Betsy inside a room on the second floor looking out on Main Street. The hot water came and he went to the bathroom on the first floor. He stepped into the cast-iron tub and almost scalded himself. It was a half-hour before he decided he had soaked and scrubbed and rinsed long enough. It had been three weeks since he'd had a proper hot bath.

Back in his room he realized that if he was going to stay in town for a while to learn all he could about his two targets, he'd need some new town clothes. Tomorrow morning he'd see what he could do as a farrier in town and make a little bit of money. He'd talk with the blacksmith and find out what he thought about competition. Most blacksmiths hated shoeing horses.

A little after six o'clock that evening he heard gunshots and looked out his window to see eight riders galloping through town and firing pistols in the air. That was when he decided it must be Saturday and the cowboys were in town to blow off steam. The riders came back walking their mounts and dropping off at their favorite saloons. There were plenty to choose from. Wade could see six from his window. One was much larger than the others and had two stories on top of the saloon.

He remembered that the café closed at seven, so he went down and had two pieces of pie and coffee, then looked for a barbershop. Being Saturday night one was open. He stepped into the chair and asked for a regular haircut. His hair had grown long, touching his neck. Then he decided to check out some of the saloons. He didn't want to ask about any names yet. First he'd see what he could learn just by watching and listening. The town might even have a weekly newspaper.

The first watering hole he went into was one step above a barrel saloon. It had sawdust on the floor. The bar on one side was a slab of rough lumber that sat on two barrels. There was no mirror, only two poker tables, and no other gambling games. Three men stood at the bar and all turned and stared at him. He nodded and left as quickly as he could walk.

The second saloon was fancy, with a mahogany bar polished to a brilliant shine and two barkeeps with clean shirts. There were ten or twelve card tables, two three-card-monte tables, and another one set up for playing dice. Fifteen or twenty men sat at the tables or stood at the bar. There was a little stage just big enough for a scarred and battered upright piano. A man sat there plunking out a popular song of the day about how this cowboy had lost his true love. The floor was solid wood which had been varnished until it shone. About half the men were cowboys with tall hats, leather vests, and six-guns slung low on their hips.

He went to the bar and asked for a beer. It cost fifteen cents. Outrageous but he paid without comment. Then he listened. The talk was muted. He wandered around the card tables watching the play. Not a lot of money on the tables.

He tried to remember what the two men he hunted looked like. It had been almost five years ago. One was left-handed, maybe five feet ten or so, and on the chubby side. He was the one who had worn the black patch over his left eye. He might have a glass eye by now.

The other one was shorter, slender, black hair, and clean-shaven. That was all he could remember about him. The shortest one had been the Captain. That would make him Captain John Brewer. So the heavy one had to be

Anderson. Nobody in the saloon came near to answering those descriptions. He left the place and passed the general store, which was still Saturday-night open. They called it the East Bend Mercantile. He needed supplies, but he could get them later. No, maybe he wouldn't be doing much more traveling if the two killers were still in town. He saw a newspaper on the counter: the *East Bend Clarion*. Four pages. He paid a nickel for the paper and put it under his arm. Near by were containers of hard candy. He picked out a dozen and put them on the counter.

The clerk came off a stool at the back and smiled.

'Yes sir, the old sweet tooth, right? You've got a dime's worth there. I'll put them in a sack for you.'

The clerk was young, maybe seventeen. Wade guessed he might be the son of the owner. He gave the clerk a dime and asked how many people lived in East Bend.

'Let's see, we had six move in last

week. Then a new baby, so that should bring us up to two thousand four hundred and twelve.'

'Looks like a nice little town.'

'Mostly ranches around here. Lots of cattle country. Heard something about a railroad that could run a spur line south from the Union Pacific but it for sure won't come through East Bend.'

Wade waved a goodbye and went out the door. In the splash of light from the lanterns inside the store he looked at the front page of the paper. A headline jumped out at him. RUDY ANDERSON ELECTED MAYOR. Wade hurried back to his hotel room so he could read the paper. Was it the same Rudy Rudolph Anderson he had been hunting for the past five years?

9

In his hotel room Wade struck a kitchen match, lit the coal-oil lamp, and then turned down the wick so it wouldn't smoke. After putting the lamp on the dresser, he spread out the weekly newspaper on top, and read the lead story about the new mayor.

> Rudolph B. 'Rudy' Anderson, long-time proprietor of the East Bend Mercantile, was elected East Bend mayor in last Tuesday's election, beating out the incumbent, Harold Maiden, by the count of 132 to 96. The county registrar of voters reported that only 340 men were registered to vote. Only 228 of those voted, or sixty-seven per cent. The registrar said this was better than on the last city election where only

thirty-seven per cent voted.

Mayor Anderson takes over his official duties from Mayor Maiden on Monday. Mayor Maiden served two two-year terms. The election campaigning was more spirited and vocal than our mayoral elections have been in many years.

Mayor Anderson has been a resident of East Bend for a little over four years. He arrived here after the war and soon bought the general store. He renamed it the East Bend Mercantile and brought in new goods and built up a thriving grocery section, asking nearby farmers to bring in fruits and vegetables in season for him to sell. He also originated the sale of bread at his store baked by area housewives.

Mayor Anderson has made no comments on his election other than to say he's proud to be mayor of our town. He is married and his wife, Millicent, is an East

Bend girl, daughter of Howard and Martha North. The Andersons have two children, a son and a daughter.

Welcome Mayor Anderson.

Wade stared at the story and read it a second time. He used his knife and cut out the story and put it on the dresser top. This was something he hadn't thought of. Anderson was a pillar of the community. The idea of finding him and shooting him dead where he stood had rapidly lost its appeal. What was he going to do with Anderson? The man was still a murderer.

He could shoot Anderson almost anytime. But that would leave a grieving widow and two fatherless children. He could confront him, tell him to leave town and if he didn't he could talk to the newspaper editor and tell him about Anderson's real background during the war. Again, that would be damaging to the wife and her children. Just what should he do about Anderson?

Wade looked at his watch. Nine o'clock. He read the article again. Then he went for a fifteen-minute walk up and down the business section of East Bend. It was only two blocks long, with frequent gaps in the businesses on both sides of the street. That meant empty places in the boardwalks. He nearly fell down when he stepped into the void at the first vacant stretch. He made mental notes of the business firms. There was a harness-maker and a blacksmith at the far end, near what also must be a livery stable. He found a millinery shop, a tinware store, a small hardware, a leather goods, and another hotel. About an average mix of stores for a small Western town. There were also saloons. He counted six or eight. There was one huge one with an upstairs.

When he finished his circuit of the two-block-long Main Street business section, he went back into the Bend Hotel, the best one in town. It should be: he had to pay a dollar fifty for a room. He had signed in for three nights. Now it looked like he might be here longer. The lobby was better than most, with upholstered furniture, a polished hardwood floor, three fancy lamps, and a stack of magazines and newspapers. He went up to his second story room still wondering what to do about Anderson. He had no idea. He'd go meet the man tomorrow at his store. That might give him a clue.

⋆ ⋆ ⋆

Rudy Anderson closed his mercantile and carried the last lamp back to his small office in the rear of the store. He still had a smile after two days of being the mayor. He laughed softly. Oh yes! Mayor of the largest town in Jewell County. There wasn't much public money running around but there was some.

He sat in the chair at his desk and counted the day's receipts. Not a big bundle, but enough to stay open and make plans to expand. Either that or simply buy the leather-and-harness shop next door. First he'd have to talk Joe Welton into selling. Maybe he could buy out Joe and keep him on as manager and saddlemaker.

He couldn't keep from grinning. He'd come a long way in just four years. Those three years in the army and then riding with the Captain had been the low point. The move west had been his salvation. Here he was mayor, store owner, member of the Baptist Church, and a pillar of the community. So why did he want to get involved with Captain Brewer again? Money. Yes, the amount of money they could make in a few months was amazing. If everything went right. Not a lot could go wrong. He would be insulated from the actual business involved. He'd just provide some capital.

They had been talking about it for over a year now, and work was under way. It all had started when a friend of

Brewer had written them from Chicago. He said it was as foolproof as possible. And the product would never go out of style or demand.

Anderson put the greenbacks in piles of ones, twos, fives and tens. No twenties today. Not many people in town had that much money. The monetary crash of 1857 was still causing pain, but the country was coming out of it. Still, the average working man earned about $200 a year. Of course, what money people had went a long way. Prices in his store were remarkably low. He kept them that way. But if the big plan worked out, he could quit worrying about scraping the barrel, move to Topeka or some other big city, do some investing, and live the life of a prosperous gentleman.

He sighed. It had been a hard-won position that he had right now. He had come to town with the $2,000 in gold and nothing else. Captain Brewer had gone to Topeka to read for the law. He'd been part-way through in

Tennessee before the war and wanted to continue and get a Kansas license.

This town had been a happenstance. He'd been heading for California when he came into East Bend. He had been on the trail for a week and was hungry and tired. He took a room at the hotel, had a bath and then a big dinner. He looked around the little town and decided to stay for a while. He would find a job somewhere, maybe a clerk in a store.

* * *

Wade Tretter started his first full day in East Bend with a big breakfast at the Kansas Café. When he left it he looked back the way he came and crashed into a girl on the boardwalk. They both fell down. Wade scrambled to his feet and helped her to stand. She was so beautiful he couldn't believe it, and well-dressed. He apologized and asked if he could treat her to a cup of coffee to make up for his clumsiness. She at first refused, then when he kept talking she laughed softly, and said she thought it might be all right after all.

They had coffee and talked. He found out she was the schoolteacher in town and had been to Normal School for her training. He was enraptured with the girl.

'My name is Wade Tretter and I'm from Missouri.' He looked at her and she smiled. It made her face blossom and brought a twinkle to her eyes.

'I'm Rebecca Lewton. My friends call me Becky.' She closed her eyes for a moment, then looked back at him with that wonderful smile. 'Wade, I hope that you'll be one of my friends.'

He felt his heart race faster and he couldn't believe his ears. She was so wonderful, so pretty. Wow! He gulped and nodded, not able to say a word for a minute. When he looked up he smiled. 'Rebecca, I would be honored to be able to call you Becky. I know that we've just met but I know deep in my heart that you're the girl I'm going to marry. Could I have your permission to come courting?'

'Courting? Marry? Now you are moving too fast and getting way ahead of yourself.' Her small frown vanished and dimples poked into both cheeks. 'But you are sweet and thoughtful. You know that you'll have to ask my father about courting.'

'I'll be glad to do that.'

'My father is our town's doctor. Even though I'm eighteen now he has allowed only two men to come courting. He's very strict. I have one brother and Father is quite overprotective. What do you do for a living?'

'I'm a farrier. Work for myself. I don't work with any blacksmith or stable, but I might here in town.'

'A farrier is honorable work. The last man who asked to come courting was a barman in a saloon. My father threw him out of his office.'

'Wow. I guess I better get a real job before I go see him.'

'If you do come courting it would

have to be on Sunday afternoons. That's what my father tells me. Oh, I'm a teacher, one of two at our school here.'

'At eighteen you're a teacher?

'I went to Normal School for a year. Lots of teachers are young.' She looked at a clock on the wall. 'Oh, dear. I'm going to be late. I have to run. With no school this summer I'm volunteering at our brand-new East Bend library. It's just down the street.'

She slid out of the booth and stood. He jumped to his feet. Becky held out her hand.

'Mr Tretter, it's been interesting meeting you.' She paused as he held on to her hand. 'I . . . I hope you come see me at the library.' Then she turned and hurried out the door.

* * *

Back almost four years ago, when Rudy Anderson hit town and decided to stay, it took him three days to find a job. By the end of the third day everyone in town knew the new guy from Tennessee was looking for work. He went into the general store without much hope.

The man who owned the store was in his seventies. He'd had the place for ten years, since the very first store went up at the cross roads that turned into a town. His eyes were starting to fail and he needed help.

'Can't afford to pay you much, son,' Stanley Orfronbach said. 'But it just might be a chance for you to learn the business. Know I can't last forever.'

Anderson had taken the job at two dollars a week and was delighted to get the work. He found a board-and-room house where he could get a bed and two meals a day for three dollars a week. Which meant he had to dip into his almost $2,000 in gold pieces hidden in his gear.

The second day of job-hunting he had borrowed a twenty-dollar gold piece from his saddle bank and bought two pairs of trousers, a new pair of jeans, three shirts, some underwear, and socks. Then he had felt more confident when job hunting.

At first on the job at the general store he swept out, washed down the boardwalk in front of the store every morning with two buckets of water, and did a lot of stocking. Gradually he learned where the merchandise was, how it was priced, and he began to wait on customers. Mr Orfronbach didn't let him handle money for almost a month. Then he let him wait on customers and make change. After a year he knew the business better than the owner did. Now and then the old man didn't make it into work until noon and sometimes not at all,

Just after two and a half years working at the store, Mr Orfronbach called Rudy over to the chair where he spent most of his time these days. 'Rudy, this isn't working out. I'm not doing my share. How much am I paying you now?'

'Five dollars a week, Mr Ofronbach.'

'Pity, not enough. You have any way to borrow money? The bank here in town knows you?'

'I do know Mr Marshall at the bank.'

'I'm wearing out, Rudy. I'm falling apart. Can't stand the work any more. I want to sell the store to you. You've earned it these past two years. I figure I do about five hundred dollars a year in profits after paying both of our wages. If I asked you for fifteen hundred dollars, you think you could borrow that much somewhere?'

Rudy stood there stunned. The value was there, and the $1,500 made it a steal. He still had over $1,900 in his gear.

'Mr Orfronbach, let me talk to the bank and to some friends. I think I can come up with the money.'

The store-owner nodded. 'If we can do a deal, I'll move back to Topeka.'

The store took on an entirely different look to him that afternoon as Rudy flew around waiting on customers, giving a big smile and a handshake to everyone. This was the answer to all of his hopes. He had a growing family to take care of. The store would be his lifeboat, down a muddy river. That first year in town he had courted Millicent North and after six months married her. Now they had a son and a daughter.

The rest of that day he had been euphoric. No longer would they have to live from one pay-day to the next. He'd be a merchant with a store and an inventory and he could make $600 or $700 a year in profit. He could buy a house, or build one, and settle down to becoming an important man in the community.

* * *

In March of 1869 Captain John Brewer came to East Bend. He and Anderson had corresponded over the four years they had been apart. Brewer had finished his law studies and been certified as a registered lawyer in the

State of Kansas. He had been working in Topeka and Chicago on an on-and-off basis with some old friends from the army. Now he said his friends there wanted a branch office, as they called it, farther west. Somewhere where the law people would not be harrying them all the time. Brewer needed some money to close the deal.

Brewer had written to Rudy. He had a law practice in Topeka but now he had a new interest. Rudy said he'd help him get established in East Bend and he could help finance the new venture.

Brewer arrived, set up a law office, and hung out his shingle. He had little work because the lawyer who had been in town five years got most of the cases and legal work. Brewer hated the old-time lawyer. Brewer needed a good local law practice and to become an established part of the community before he went into the new phase of his business, which he called 'The Plan'.

A month after Brewer arrived, a curious thing happened. The established lawyer, whose name was Lawrence Larson, was involved in a buggy accident. One of the wheels fell off his rig as he was trotting down Graveyard Hill at the edge of town. The rig crashed and pulled the horse over a steep embankment. The horse had a broken leg and had to be put down. The buggy was ruined and lawyer Larson escaped with a concussion, a broken arm and some minor cuts and bruises.

A week later a small barn and stable on the lawyer's place at the edge of town caught on fire late one night and burned to the ground killing his prize riding horse inside. The sheriff investigated but could find no cause of the fire.

The next day a letter arrived from Topeka for Larson. He picked it up at the post office in the mercantile. It was in a firm feminine hand:

My Dear Mr Larson.
I am a friend and I suggest strongly that you leave your situation there in East Bend. I understand that you have had some serious accidents lately. There is a strong chance that more accidents will befall you and your wife and two small children if you remain in East Bend. I will consider this matter closed if you relocate your family and your business within a week of the day you receive this letter.

It was not signed. He looked at the postmark on the envelope. It had been mailed a week before from Topeka. He scowled.

He had wondered about the wheel coming off the buggy and then the fire. Both had to be deliberate attempts to run him out of town. He could go to the sheriff. Show him the letter. But what could the sheriff do? There was no hard evidence or threat.

That night just after dark, a lone rider on a black horse rode past the Larson home and fired five shots from a six-gun through the front window. Most of the shots missed those inside, but his wife took one round in her thigh. Doctor Lewton pulled out the slug and said there would be no lasting damage.

After the doctor left Larson told his wife the whole story, about the accidents that were not accidents, and how someone had written him a letter suggesting that he leave town at once. His wife cried and said she didn't want to leave. He said, if they stayed she would still have her friends, but she would also be wearing widow's weeds.

He fumed for three days and then told his wife they were moving. He had friends in Topeka who had offered him a job in their law firm. He'd have a guaranteed salary and he would be safe from these planned attacks on him. They were gone three days later, taking their buggy and most of their possessions. They drove south to the first town that had stagecoach service.

The day Larson left John Brewer moved his law practice from the small office he had been using to the larger, better situated one Larson had used near the bank. He put out a dignified sign: JOHN BREWER, ESQ. ATTORNEY AT LAW, and settled into working with most of the clients whom Larson had serviced.

John Brewer, now thirty-three years old, stood five feet five inches tall, a little shorter than average for the day. He had put on a few pounds since his army days. His hair was still black as soot and there was a sparkle in his eye. Women liked his dark good looks. He had never married. Now, with his law office established here, he went visiting to some of the business firms in town. One of them was the struggling print shop. He knew that in most small towns that had newspapers, the proprietors supplemented their income with job printing. Here the print shop had arrived in town well before a newspaper could survive and still did the print work for the town, with an agreement with the paper that it would not do job printing.

But now beef prices were down, the ranchers were short on funds, and the whole town had suffered. The print shop almost went broke. John Brewer arrived at the right moment. He checked the print shop, saw the books, and offered to buy out the printer at a low price.

'Your press looks like it came from England on the Mayflower,' Brewer said. 'Your stock of paper is so low you'd have to order it out of Denver before you could turn a wheel. I'll give you six hundred dollars for the whole thing. Your building, your printing operation, and your accounts receivable.'

Grant Tinker almost fell over himself shaking hands with Brewer. He had never expected to be able to sell his business, let alone come out of it with six hundred dollars.

'Mr Brewer, you've just bought yourself a printing plant.'

'Can you have all of your personal stuff out of here by tonight?'

The printer was out of the shop by noon and rode out heading for the nearest stage connection to the south the next day. Brewer hand printed a sign and put it on the outside door: *Under new Management. Closed a week for inventory and restocking.*

That should do it. He could run a press and he did know about typesetting. If things went right he wouldn't need to do much actual job printing to stay open and keep the new press working.

The modern press was on its way. It would come on the Union Pacific Railroad as far as Julesburg up in Nebraska. Actually it would be offloaded two stops before Julesburg at the small town of Brule, Nebraska. A man riding with the press would hire a rig there and find a wagon route down from the rail line into Kansas and right into East Bend. It would be about eighty miles and at least half of it would not have improved roads. The rig would have to go cross-country in an almost due south route. As soon as the new press came, they could get into production.

Brewer rubbed his hands together in excitement. A lot of the outfit's success would depend on his contacts. He had been trained on a press like the new one coming for three months in Topeka. Nothing would go wrong. With the press would come the ink and the paper that was twenty-five per cent linen and seventy-five per cent long-grain cotton. He had been in town for three months and had rented a house and furnished it. He ate out most of the time. The problem was, there wasn't the variety of dishes served here that he had become used to in Topeka.

By moving their operation this far into the west, they figured they could work out of this location for more than a year. They had maintained operations in Topeka for six months. Now they would do the job more cleanly, with better salesmen and a smarter overall operation.

10

The first thing Wade did his second day in East Bend, after breakfast, was to walk Betsy down to the blacksmith's forge at the Wagon Wheel livery stable at the edge of town. He met the smith, a medium-sized man with well-developed shoulders and arms. The forge was not fired and the man was working his stable duties. He looked up from a well-worn notebook.

'Yeah, the new kid in town. Put up your nag for a couple of days?'

'Maybe longer. Hear you do farrier work.'

'When I got to.'

'I'm a farrier looking for a job. You got any rental horses that need hoof work?'

The smith settled back in the beat-up chair behind a desk made of a plank over two feed barrels. He eyed Wade a minute.

'Look young, you have any experience?'

'Figure I've done about a thousand shoes over the past two years. Working my way west from Missouri.'

'A thousand?'

'Probably more. I hear you got kicked a short time ago.'

'Yeah. Blasted old swayback. One little nail went in wrong and she got her dander up.' He squinted up at Wade. 'You any good?'

'Some say. I'm smart enough to keep the nails out of the inner hoof where it hurts.'

'You trim the hoofs and all?'

'If they need it.'

'Got your own kit of tools?'

'I have.'

The man heaved up to his feet and stared hard at Wade. He had a mustache and thinning hair on top. He wore an unbuttoned blue denim shirt with cut-off sleeves.

'You got a name?' He held out his hand. 'I'm Frank Kearney.'

'Wade Tretter.' Wade took his hand and shook it.

'I like an honest handshake.' Kearney nodded. 'Tell you what, Wade. I've got two mares out there in the rental corral that need shoes. You trim their hoofs and slick them up and put on new shoes on both of them, and I'll pay you a quarter for each hoof. Then if I like your work, and the way you handle the stock, I'll let you work out of here and you can charge what you want.'

'I can use the forge if I need to?'

'If it's hot.'

'Show me those mares.'

The first mare had thrown a front shoe. All four hoofs were overgrown and disrupting the fit of the shoes. He took off three, cleaned out the hoofs, cut them back into shape and put on the new shoes the smith handed him. Three fit well. The fourth he had to pound a little on the cold anvil to get it into shape.

Kearney watched him put on the first two shoes, then went back to his books.

He rented a rig to someone, then took in three saddle horses and put them in stalls.

It was almost ten o'clock before Wade finished the last mare's shoes. He told Kearney, who went out to the corral to look at them.

'Be damned. That's as good a shoeing job as I've ever seen done. You're good at your work, son. Who taught you?'

'My pa, when I was fourteen.'

'What do you usually charge?'

'Twenty-five to thirty-five a shoe.'

'I been charging fifty cents. You can do the same. Too much work for a quarter. I'll give you four dollars for the eight shoes you put on for me. Worth it. Spread the word that you're working here on shoes. You'll get some business. Best go up to the general store, the mercantile, the mayor calls it, and tell him you're in business down here. Men usually get their shoes up there, then come down here. Anderson keeps a keg or two of all sizes of shoes.'

‘That I can do.’

Kearney peeled four bills off a roll from his pocket. ‘You take greenbacks?’

‘Most everyone does now,’ Wade said. ‘Five years ago the greenback was down to about thirty cents on the dollar. Now it’s back to a hundred per cent.’

‘Good. Now, two more things. Leave your horse here at no charge. You take care of her. Put her in the corral. All I ask is that you pay for the oats, and if I run short on horses sometime, I get to rent her out. I’ll split the fee with you. Sound fair?’

‘Yes.’

‘The other thing is you should stop by the newspaper and tell the editor you’re in town and working your farrier trade down here at the livery. He should run a small story on you. Can’t hurt.’

Wade went back to Betsy, gave her half a scoop of oats, took her saddle off, then brushed her down. When she finished eating, he led her back to the corral, took her bridle off, and let her go. She looked at him a moment, then pranced round the corral twice before stopping at the water trough.

After that he put his kit of farrier tools in the first stall and hung his saddle on a peg. He had taken the last gold coins and the $500 in bills out of their hiding-place last night when he took the rest of his gear and what was left of his food and camping things into the hotel room.

A short walk later he learned that the newspaper was a two-man affair. One handled the editorial and the advertising, the other the typesetting and printing. The full-sized four pages kept them busy all week and they published on Thursday. The editor's name was Neil Russell. He had on a white shirt with the sleeves rolled up, a loose tie, and thick glasses. He sipped at a cup of coffee, offered one to Wade, then smiled.

'I'm Wade Tretter, just got in town and I'm doing farrier work down at the livery.'

'So you talked to our man down

there and got the farrier concession? Good. Kearney was never too good shoeing a horse anyway. Yeah, I can run a story on it. You aiming to stay a while? You should get a lot of business once word gets around. Now, I've got to get two more stories done before noon. Good to meetcha.'

Wade shook his hand again and went out to the street. As he walked toward his hotel he saw a hand-lettered sign in a store window. It said: East Bend Library. He grinned, pushed open the door, and went inside.

It almost looked like a library. One wall had shelves that were about half-filled with books. Another book-rack was under construction on the floor on the other side of the room. A figure on hands and knees swung a hammer followed by a shout of pain.

'Oh, no. I hit my finger.'

He looked closely as the figure turned. It was Becky Lewton. She grinned. 'Sorry about the outburst. It hurts.' She sat on the floor, her dress billowing round her covering her legs and feet. 'Wade, do you know how to pound a nail?'

'Done that a time or two, Miss Lewton.' He knelt on the floor beside her, looked at the offending nail, and the hammer she still held. He took the weapon from her, angled the nail a little so it would hit the shelf, and pounded it in with three hits.

'Wow, that looked so easy,' Becky said. She laughed and shook her head. 'Some things I'm better at than others. Could you get this shelf all nailed in place for me? I'm such a clumsy carpenter.'

He watched her. She was so beautiful. He'd never seen a girl like Becky before. Her smile made him want to jump over the moon. She let her dimples pop in and he laughed to cover his nervousness.

'Just takes a little practice. This is the shelf and it goes right here,' he said adjusting the board against the upright.

'Yes, exactly.' She watched him, her

eyes bright. She was delighted that he had come by. She would keep him here as long as she could. She wondered whether he got a job yet and if he was really going to test the old bear in his den — her father.

He pounded in more nails, secured that shelf, then a second one.

'Two more shelves and we can stand them up,' she said.

Wade nodded. That would complete the five shelf section. He picked up the next shelf board and put it in place. 'Yes, two more shelves and then we go to dinner. Or do the people in town call the noon meal lunch?'

'Lunch, mostly.' She frowned. 'I don't know, about lunch, I mean. I'm glad you came by. I'd never have had that shelf done by noon.' She lifted her brows. He even liked the way she looked when she frowned.

She brightened. 'Yes, I can go to lunch, but I have to pay for my own meal. Usually I don't eat much at noon.'

A woman came in the door and smiled at the two working on the shelving.

'I wonder if you have anything by Charles Dickens?' she asked looking at Becky.

Becky brightened and stood effortlessly from where she had been sitting on the wooden floor.

'You're in luck, Mrs Baldwin. We just got in a copy of *Oliver Twist*. Charles Dickens wrote it between 1837 and 1839 when he lived in London. It's right over here. Just sign a card for it and you get to keep it for thirty days. Did you know it was first published chapter by chapter in a London newspaper? That's how Dickens made his living back then. Later it was a book.'

'I want to thank you for starting the library. I know you have one at school, but this will be more for adults. Thanks so much.'

She took the book and went out the door.

'Now that's what it's all about, having a library to furnish the public with books. It makes me feel warm and happy all over.'

Wade pounded the last nail in, stood and tipped the five-shelf section upright, and pushed it against an open wall.

'Perfect,' Becky said. 'Now all we need to do is paint it.'

'Lunch first,' Wade said.

The meal was amazing, just sitting across from her and watching her pick at her small sandwich and a bowl of fruit. He had a ham sandwich with lots of lettuce, cheese, and mustard on it.

'So I told this woman that we were going to have a library and she brought in four boxes of books. All but two I registered in, gave them numbers and put them on the shelf. It gave us a start. We now have three hundred and twelve books. Before the end of the year we hope to have over two thousand.'

Becky lifted her brows and sighed. 'Oh dear. I've done it again. My father says that I run off at the mouth at every possible opportunity. Do you think that's true?' She looked up at him and he couldn't wash the silly grin off his face. He was flustered and nervous around this beautiful girl. He didn't know how to talk to her, or what to say, or even how to be just common well-mannered. He realized he knew almost nothing about girls.

He cleared his throat and blinked. 'Becky, I don't think you talk too much. I love to listen to you.'

The waitress brought slips of paper to the table showing how much each owed. Becky had told her to bring separate checks. Wade reached for her check but she beat him to it with a little laugh.

'Oh, no. If my father were to walk in and see us and you bought me lunch, he would be angry with me. You leave him to me.'

She smiled again and it made him forget why he was in town.

'You said you were a farrier.'

He told her about his job at the livery.

'That's wonderful. Father can't complain about that. You're a businessman, with a trade. Yes, I think he might like that. He has two horses and he loves to ride, but he's always complaining about the poor job that Mr Kearney does on the horseshoes.' She looked at the clock on the wall and scooted out of the booth. 'I have to get back to open the library.'

'I can help make more shelves if you need them,' he said.

'Oh yes, wonderful. I'll see about getting some more lumber. We could use a good lumberyard in town.'

She stood and he scrambled out after her and walked with her to the door, then back to the library half a block away. There she reached out her hand and shook his.

'Mr Tretter, it's been fun being with you today. I hope to have some more shelf lumber before five o'clock tonight.'

'I'll be there,' Wade said. Then he hurried away toward the livery. There might be somebody wanting some hoof work done. At the livery there were no customers for shoes. He brushed down Betsy again, gave her some oats, then turned her loose in the corral. He knew he had been putting it off. He took a deep breath and told Kearney he had to go up to the mercantile and tell them he was doing farrier work.

Would he see Rudy Anderson there? Would he draw his Colt and put a bullet between his eyes before he calmed down? No, he wouldn't. He wasn't wearing the gunbelt or his Colt. Both were back in his hotel room. He might not even see the owner. A clerk might talk to him. He had passed the mercantile last night when it was closed. Now he turned and went past the county sheriff's office and on two doors to the East Bend mercantile. He pulled open the door and walked inside. It was jammed with merchandise of all kinds from horse-collars to fancy women's clothes, jeans, shirts, hardware, heating-stoves, and everything a woman would need in the kitchen and the house.

He walked through the displays to a counter near the back. A man in his mid-thirties sat on a stool behind the counter reading a newspaper. He looked up. The man had to be Anderson. He didn't have the eyepatch but the left eye stared straight ahead. A glass one. He had the scar over his left eye on his forehead from a bullet graze. The Anderson he searched for had a slight limp. Was this the right man? Yes. He knew it was without waiting for the limp. He had close-cut black hair and soft, blue eyes.

'Yes sir, young man, how can I help you?'

'You Mr Anderson?'

'Indeed I am. You can call me Mayor Anderson.'

'I just took over the farrier work down at the livery. Wanted to let you know that when riders come in for horseshoes, I'll be on hand most of the time to put on the new shoes.'

'Good. That's fine news. Kearney was never very good at shoeing a mount. You charge same as he did?'

'Yes sir. Fifty cents a hoof. I been shoeing horses since I was fourteen. My pa taught me to do it.'

'That's fine. I just received a new keg of shoes, most sizes. But then if they don't fit exactly, you have the forge down there to whip them into the right shape.'

'Thank you, Mayor. My name is Wade Tretter and I plan on being around town for some time. Congratulations on your election.'

'Yes, thank you. I'll help spread the word about your services.'

Wade looked around, saw nothing that he needed, waved, then walked out of the store. He had held his temper. The old hatred had surfaced and almost burst out but he had kept a tight lock on it. There he was staring at the man who had killed his pa and stood by while one of his men killed his ma. He wanted to strangle the man. But he couldn't. He didn't have any idea how he could punish this killer and still not devastate the man's family. How was he going to punish this killer?

He kicked at the boardwalk and headed back to the livery. Tomorrow he'd take his kit of farrier tools, display them on the boardwalk in front of the mercantile, and let riders know that he was in business. Yes, that would work. Tomorrow. He wished that he could go courting Becky. First he had to see her doctor father. That would have to wait a few days.

11

Wade figured it was his third or fourth day in town when he paid more attention to the signs on the stores and offices. One he had missed entirely. Now he stood to the side and read the hand-lettered sign again.

JOHN BREWER ATTORNEY AT LAW.
Licensed by the State of Kansas.

For a moment he was stunned. He stepped to the front wall of the store next to the lawyer's office and leaned there frowning. Was it possible? It was the same name. Was this the John Brewer who had ridden up to his pa and put a .44 slug through his heart back in Missouri? He stood there thinking it through. Bert Daniels said that both Anderson and Brewer were in East Bend. Did he mean it? The name was the same. It could be. A sudden flare of the old hatred surged through his brain and his body. Two hits in a row. It could be the same Brewer. Had Daniels said anything about Brewer wanting to be a lawyer? He couldn't remember. He hurried back to the hotel and dug out the small notebook in which he had kept track of everything. He read the pages he'd written the day his parents died.

The description of John Brewer, then called the Captain:

> The Captain looks to be about five feet five inches tall and maybe a hundred and forty pounds. Shortest of the four. Clean-shaven with slick black hair. His face is long and thin like a bat.

So, a short man with black hair and a thin face. An urgency he hadn't felt in months tore at him. He had to find out for sure and he had to do it right now. He walked back to the lawyer's door

hotel and put on a clean shirt and his best pair of trousers, washed off his boots, polished them with a rag, then scrubbed his face and his hands until they were as clean as cucumbers. He combed his hair. He looked in the mirror. A shave. He had to have a shave. Always lots of fun in cold water but he didn't want to take the time to get hot from the kitchen. He labored for ten minutes scraping the three days of growth off his face, then he felt ready.

The walk of a block to the doctor's office seemed like a long one to him. He had no idea whether the doctor was in or out, seeing a patient, or whether he needed an appointment, but he barged in the door, and looked at four people sitting in the waiting-room. A desk stood in the far corner It held a number of folders and a woman sat behind it. She looked up.

'Yes, young man; how may we help you?' She was about forty, plump, with a pretty face, and soft brown hair cut short. She wore a dress and over that a white smock.

Wade walked up to her and spoke softly.

'I'd like to see Dr Lewton.'

She glanced up. 'You don't look sick. What's your problem?'

'I just need to talk to him.'

She frowned for a moment, then her round face lit up and she smiled. Then she spoke softly so no one else could hear. 'Oh, yes. You're that young farrier in town. I've seen you at the library. This wouldn't have anything to do with Rebecca, now, would it?'

'Yes, ma'am it would. I'm Wade Tretter.'

'Good. The doctor is busy with a patient, but he needs a break from his hard work. I'll get him a glass of lemonade and tell him you're here. He's always interested in seeing possible suitors for his daughter. Sit down and I'll call you in a few minutes.' He sat and she vanished through a door that led into the back of the building.

Wade watched the others in the waiting-room. There was a mother with a three- or four-year-old son. The boy was crying softly and the mother kept touching his forehead. An old Indian man sat away from the others. He wore white man's clothes but had an Indian robe pulled tightly around him. There were no feathers in his hair and his face was burned a deep reddish brown.

Near Wade sat a young woman, maybe twenty-five. She squirmed on the chair and he saw that she was pregnant but trying to hide the fact with a loose dress and a robe over that. None of the people in the room made eye contact with him. This was not a place for socializing or making idle talk.

Only a few minutes after the doctor's helper went into the back she came out and looked at a folder.

'Mr Tretter. The doctor will see you.' She looked at the others in the room. 'Doctor is a little busy right now, but he'll see each of you just as quickly as possible. Mrs Ralston, you and your son will be next.'

Wade stood and walked over to the door the woman held open for him. He felt his knees go soft and almost give out. Now was not the time to turn into a yellow-belly and run out the front door. That idea had come to him more than once as he waited. The woman led him down a narrow hall to a room with an open door. It was an office and den. Inside behind a small desk sat a man with spectacles, an eye-shade and a white jacket such as many doctors were starting to wear. He sipped at a glass of lemonade.

'Mr Tretter. Sit down; we need to have a talk.'

Doctor Lewton was about fifty with short red hair thinning on top. He wore a white waist-length white jacket, white shirt, and a tie. A stethoscope hung around his neck. He had a ruddy complexion, sharp, piercing blue eyes, thick brows and he was clean-shaven. He had a thin white two-inch-long scar on his left cheek, and his shoulders and arms looked well developed, as if he had been a wrestler or long-distance swimmer.

'Tretter. I hear from Grace that you're interested in coming courting Rebecca. You know she's barely eighteen?'

'Yes, I know. I talked with her in the library. She's an amazing young lady and I'd like your permission to come courting so we can get to know each other better.'

'You have a trade, young man?'

'Yes sir, I'm a farrier. I'm working out of the livery but independent from it. I've been making my living as a farrier for the past four years.'

'You have a bit of an accent I'm not familiar with.'

'I grew up in Missouri, southern part.'

'Yes.' The doctor fiddled with a paper on his desk, then frowned when he looked up. 'What are your intentions toward my daughter?'

'Sir, I believe strongly that she is the

woman that I am going to marry. I think it will take a six-month courtship for me to prove myself to her and to you, and for us both to become properly acquainted with each other.'

'Hmmmmm. At least you're honest about it. Do you think Rebecca is attractive?'

'No sir. I think she's the most beautiful woman that I've ever laid eyes on.'

'Well now. We do have one thing in common there.' He put the paper down and picked it up again. 'You planning on being a farrier all your life?'

'No sir. It's what my pa taught me before Rebel raiders killed him at the end of the war on our farm in Missouri. I can earn what I need this way. I've always thought I'd like to get into the retail business — some kind of a store.'

'Yes. Being a merchant is an honorable trade. How old are you, young man?'

'Going on nineteen, sir. Come August fourteen I turn nineteen.'

'I heard about those raiders. Did some doctoring for the north during the war. They probably killed your mother too, right?'

Wade nodded.

'I'm sorry. How did you escape?'

'I was gone hunting when they came. I saw them. Pa told me to hide if I saw strangers riding into the place. So I did. Hid in the grass and they never saw me.'

'Good for you. We heard about hundreds of cases like that all along the line between the north and the south. Quantrell was the worst of the lot. Never could understand how they let him get away.'

'Yes sir.'

The doctor tipped up the glass of lemonade and drained it, then put it down on his desk. 'Well, I have some patients to see. You may come courting once a week on Sunday night. I suppose that you'll be attending our church services on Sunday morning. I'd look on favorably if you do. So, Sunday it is at six-thirty to eight. No later. Most likely I or my wife will be sitting in with you. Thank you and good day.'

Wade stood. 'Thank you sir. I'll be there Sunday.'

He went out the door to the waiting-room. The nurse, Grace, motioned him over to her desk.

'So?' she asked softly.

'Sunday nights.' Wade couldn't suppress a grin.

'Good,' she said, just to him. 'Now be sure you go to church services every Sunday morning and shake the doctor's hand so he knows you're there. That's first on his list. You'll find out more of his requirements as you go along. Good luck.'

He hurried out the door and let out a small yell of delight, then ran up the block to the library. Rebecca had just checked out a book to a mother and her son. When she finished she looked up and her smile brightened when she saw him. She brushed back her hair with a hand and watched him.

'You're smiling,' she said. 'Good news?'

'I talked to your father.'

'Yes?'

'I get to come courting Sunday nights from six-thirty to eight.'

'Wonderful!' She reached out and caught his hand. 'I'm so glad. I'm delighted. He must like you. In the past courting has only been for an hour.'

'But just one night a week?'

'That's what Papa says. He says if a young man is really interested in me he'll come just once a week.'

'At least I can see you here. Any more bookshelves you need made?'

She laughed. 'Not right now. I have more than enough.'

Wade stood there holding her hand. He was thrilled by her touch. He never wanted to let go.

She motioned to her hand with the other one. 'Hey, farrier, you have something of mine.'

He looked up, confused for the moment. Then he nodded. 'Your hand.

I'm going to put it in my pocket and keep it forever.'

She loosened her fingers and pulled them back. 'Oh, a message for you. A small boy brought it. He said that there are three horses waiting for you down at the livery. They need shoes.'

He harrumphed. 'Story of my life. I go from holding a beautiful lady's hand to going to the stable and holding a horse's hoof.' They both laughed. He waved and hurried out of the library and down the street to the livery.

The next day he found a board-and-room place at the edge of town. It was the Widow Nelson's place. She had three other boarders.

'I charge four dollars a week for two meals a day and your room. I'll do your laundry for fifty cents a week and any minor mending needed. I got my own cow so we have all the milk, cottage cheese, butter, and buttermilk we can eat. I share the milk with my neighbor since Old Maud milks out most four gallons a day. Yep, I know lots of bigger animals can milk out up to seven gallons, but Old Maud ain't no spring heifer, so we take what we get. You gonna be in town long?'

'Yes, ma'am. I intend to stay for some time. I'm a farrier down at the livery. You know anybody who needs shoes on his horses, you send them down to me. I can pay you a week in advance if that's all right.'

'Fine. I ain't trying to get rich. Just to make ends meet. My two boys ran off to California. Never hear from them. They were supposed to take care of me in my middle years.' She laughed. The Widow Nelson was short and round and had gray hair in a bun at the back of her neck. He figured she was about forty-five. She had a cackle of a laugh that he would recognize anywhere.

He moved his gear from the hotel into his room which was in front on the second floor. It had a window. The bed was a shade better than the one he'd had in the hotel. Besides the bed he had two chairs, a dresser with a mirror over the top, and a chamber pot under the bed to save him from a trip to the outhouse on cold and stormy nights. There were even a half-dozen hangers in the closet. To one side sat a stand with a porcelain washbasin, a large porcelain pitcher of water, a wash-cloth, and a fuzzy white towel.

He lay on the bed a moment reflecting. He had taken care of two of the killers, and now he knew where the other two were. He would make plans for both of them but no rush. He had found a girl he had become tremendously fond of and hoped it would lead further. He had a job that would keep him solvent and he had a board-and-room situation so his money would go further. He had been spending about three dollars a day for the hotel and eating out.

Supper at the Nelson house was served family style around a spanning table that could seat twelve. Five of them had supper that night. They had roast beef with a half-dozen different vegetables cooked in the same pot and served in a large dish. The roast beef had been cut in generous slabs and there was plenty for seconds. The bread was white and sliced thick, with fresh butter, and gallons of coffee or milk to drink. Apple butter sat in a big saucer for those wishing some and for dessert there was apple pie with a crown of sweet whipped cream.

Two of the men asked for seconds on the pie and Mrs Nelson smiled. 'Like to feed a man who likes my apple pie.'

Wade checked the other three boarders. Ken Vincent was in his forties and a clerk in a store in town. Joe Welton was in his twenties and ran the saddle-and-leather store. He came to the table and Wade could detect the faint order of cured leather on him. It was a favorite scent for Wade.

The third man, Mike Swenson, was older, maybe sixty, had a crippled right leg, and walked with a decided limp. Wade recognized him as the barber who had cut his hair the first day he was in town. The barber nodded at Wade when they sat down.

When dinner was over, Mrs Nelson put her hands on her hips. 'All right, I'm off to the kitchen. As soon as I clear here, the table is available for checker games, or dominoes. Usually I don't offer much in the way of recreation but now that there are four of you it would be two games of checkers, if'n you got the mind to.'

One game of checkers began and Wade watched. Both were good at the game. They were the two older men. The saddle-maker said he still had some work to do and drifted out. Soon Wade went up to his room and took out a new large pad of paper and put down ideas about what he could do to punish Anderson, without hurting his wife and two small children. The options were limited and for a time he thought it might be an impossible task. Anything that would really punish Anderson would also direly effect his family. He gave it up about nine o'clock and went to bed. He noted the bedframe was made of brass instead of iron. The whole headboard and posts and frame were brass and it added a touch of class in this ordinary home. He tested the mattress again and then settled down. How could be punish Anderson? The problem went around and around in his head and he figured he'd even dream about it. He did, but no solutions surfaced.

12

Rudy Anderson. He looked over the notes he had written down last night before he went to bed. Possible punishments:

Tell Anderson he knew what he did during the war and that he had seen him and his three friends kill Wade's parents in Missouri.

Make him resign as mayor.
Blackmail him into poverty.
Force him out of his business.
Shoot him dead some dark night.
Make up a Wanted poster on him and give it to the sheriff.
Make him contribute money to the library.
Send a detailed story to the local newspaper about his killings.
Harass him day and night until he went crazy.

Tell his wife so she can divorce him.
Spread rumors about him all over town.

He stared at the list. None of it really handled the problem. He was still unhappy about having to do something that would in any way harm the man's family. He gave up and went to breakfast downstairs. The Widow Nelson had flapjacks and bacon for them with an egg on a three-stack, hot maple syrup, butter, coffee, and apple-sauce to polish it off.

'Usual I'd have grated potatoes fried up like cakes, but I ran out of time this morning,' she said. 'Overslept. You'll have to make do. I'll bring you all the hotcakes you can eat.'

Wade settled for six, four strips of bacon, and then hurried down to the livery as he did most mornings. There were three horses there whose owners had ordered new shoes all around. He inspected them, went to the mercantile and picked up shoes to fit and worked on the three mounts most of the morning. When he finished he had earned six dollars. Old Gus had made the riders pay in advance for the work and he handed over the six greenbacks to Wade, who thanked him. He brushed down Betsy, gave her a feeding of oats and let her back into the pasture. She looked like she enjoyed the rest after the long trek across two states.

Old Gus stopped Wade on his way out of the livery.

'Good day for you, young man. Six dollars is as much as I used to make in a week.'

'I appreciate your help, Gus. Can I bring you a cold beer from the saloon?'

Old Gus considered it a minute, then shook his head. 'No. Just one beer never does it for me. Then I'd leave here and go up for another one and another one. Best I just sit here and think about my animals.'

'Remember I'll shoe any of your rentals you need doing free of charge.

Least I can do.' Wade waved at the older man. 'Well, I best be moving. Got to clean up and go see a girl.'

'I heard. The doctor's daughter. Lots of men been trying for that one. Well, lots; that means two or three in a town this size. You got permission to go courting? When? On Sundays?'

'Right. What day is this?'

'Don't rightly know. Never have had a calendar. Figure if I need to know about a date somebody will tell me.'

'Fair enough. Anybody needs shoes in a rush, find a kid to hunt me down at the Widow Nelson house or the library.'

Wade hurried back to the Nelson house and cleaned up in the bowl in his room. He washed off, put on a clean shirt, and combed his hair. Shave? Maybe tomorrow. He whistled as he walked out the door and down a block to Main Street and the library.

He wanted to talk to Rebecca about Anderson but he didn't know how he could do it. No, he shouldn't. It was his problem, and no sense in making

Becky worry about it.

He found Becky putting new books in the racks. She said 'hi' to him when he came in. They had agreed not to touch each other except hold hands. She gripped his so tightly he winced, then grinned.

'Wade. So glad you came. I've been thinking about you. Do you know what day tomorrow is?'

'Been wondering.'

'Sunday.' She looked up at him, her face expectant, eyes shining. 'You can come courting!'

He frowned, his mind whirling. 'Been wondering about that. Just what do I do? I mean, I've never been courting before.'

'Silly. We mostly just sit and talk. We don't touch, not even hold hands, and usually Mother will be in the room, over on the far side pretending not to notice us.'

'A chaperone?'

'Yes. Most families I know about do it that way.'

'How long? I mean how many Sundays do I come courting?'

'At least three months. Then maybe we'll decide if we want to be together.'

'Together?'

'Get married, like you told me that first day we met when we knocked each other over on the boardwalk.'

It made him nervous now just thinking about getting married. Why did he say such a thing? He looked at Becky and at once he knew why. He wanted to grab her and hug her and . . .

'We have lots of work to do, Wade. See all these books? A man left a box of them this morning. I need to write out cards for each one, and enter them all in the register alphabetically. Then I want you to rack up the books on the shelves by the author's last name. The A authors go with the other A authors.'

'Means I got to know the alphabet?'

'Silly, you know it. You can read.'

'My ma taught me to read, write, and to do my sums and division. I like division.'

'Your ma must have been a smart woman to teach you. No school around where you grew up?'

'One, but it was too far to ride twice a day. So Ma taught me.'

They worked the rest of the afternoon, then he held her hand, said goodbye, and went to the livery. One of the rentals had thrown a shoe. He put on a new one and Old Gus grinned.

'Gol dang, you meant it, about tending to my rentals. Gol dang if you didn't.'

After supper that night at the boarding house, he went to the Last Chance saloon and had a beer, which he carried to a table in back and sat with his shoulders against the wall. It gave him a good view of everyone in the place. Maybe a beer would relax him and he could think clearly about Anderson and how to bring him to justice.

His mind felt like mush. He'd been over and over the points he wrote down last night and nothing new surfaced.

Maybe he should just shoot the man dead and not worry about his family.

His beer was only half gone when he saw two familiar figures come into the bar. They were Anderson and Brewer. It didn't surprise him that they were there together. They had known each other for four or five years. But Brewer was grinning like he'd just won a case before the Supreme Court. He bought the beers and they found a table. Their heads came close together but Brewer seemed to be doing most of the talking. Every now and then both men would laugh.

It was a happy occasion for them. They each had three beers while Wade finished his first one. He could think of nothing new for Anderson. Maybe the Indian tied-up rattlesnake torture. No. The first step would be to go see Anderson, tell him who he was and what happened in Missouri and that he was going to have justice one way or another. Then warn him not to talk to Brewer about this. His mind was made up on the first move. After that he still didn't have the slightest idea what he would do.

Tomorrow was Sunday. The mercantile would be closed along with all of the retail stores and shops. Only the hotels, the saloons and the two cafés would be open.

Tomorrow he had to go to church. Which church was no problem. Only one in town. He'd been past it a dozen times and remembered that it was the Community Church. Evidently with no ties to any denomination. The Sunday service started at eleven a.m.

* * *

Sunday morning he washed up in the bowl, put on a clean shirt, his best pair of pants, and shaved. He wished he had some bay rum to splash on his face. He'd see if they had any at the mercantile.

He stood outside the church fifteen minutes before the service time waiting to see when the good doctor and his family would arrive. They came just before eleven. The doctor, his wife, Becky, and evidently a brother about ten or twelve. They walked inside. The only one who looked at him was Becky, who gave him a quick smile, then she hurried through the doors. He walked in a short time later and took a seat in the last pew. There were about twenty people there.

He'd not been to many church services. They sang hymns. His ma used to sing hymns to him. Then a man who, he figured, was the preacher started talking. The sermon was long and repetitious and boring to Wade. Something about sin, salvation, the blood of the lamb, eternal fire, and brimstone. Then they sang again and people walked out.

He left the church first and stood outside, hoping to see Becky again. The doctor and his family came out in the middle of the group. Becky looked at him and waved, then was shunted down the sidewalk squarely between her mother and father. The brother trailed them, turned, stuck out his tongue at Wade, then hurried to catch up to the protection of his father.

Mrs Nelson watched the men eat. 'Thought you might like it,' she said, smiling. They had a whole roasted chicken with stuffing, mashed potatoes, giblet gravy from the roasting drippings, early fresh peas, some cranberry sauce, slabs of fresh-baked bread, salted butter, and coffee. For dessert she brought in cherry pie with whipped cream on top. Wade ate until he thought his shirt buttons would pop off.

'We'll have sandwiches and coffee at seven tonight in case anyone is hungry by then,' she said.

Wade went up to his room and stared out the window. Anderson. The problem plagued him. What should he do after he told Anderson that he had tracked his murdering hide down and was in town to exact justice from him and Brewer. He'd have his six-gun belt on with the loaded Colt in case Anderson figured he could get a hide-out from under the counter. If he kept one there.

Wade went for a walk. He was as jittery as a first-time mother cat with six kittens. Just talk. All they were going to do was talk. But Mrs Lewton would be there listening to every word. Careful. He had to be extremely careful what he said and how he said it.

He walked a half-mile out of town, turned around and came back. He didn't check with the livery. It was open but he never had done any farrier work on Sunday. Probably nobody would ask, unless there was a traveling man heading through. Tough luck.

Anderson.

Confrontation. He would use a soft, deadly tone that could scare the merchant. He was four years away from the war and the killings. He probably never fired his guns any more. Good.

Wade showed up at the Lewton home at 6.25 that afternoon. Becky had told him where they lived. A white-painted house with yellow trim and roses in the front yard near the white picket fence. Hard to miss.

He knocked on the door and it sprang open at once. Becky held the door, her face radiant. Dr Lewton pushed her gently out of the way as he stood there looking Wade up and down.

'Well, you came. Saw you at church this morning. You didn't sing the hymns.' He twisted his mouth. 'That's all right. I usually don't sing them myself. Come in.'

Wade let out a held-in breath. 'Good afternoon, Dr Lewton, Rebecca.' His voice sounded strange to him.

'Yes, isn't it?' Rebecca said. Her father stood aside as she motioned for Wade to follow her and she led him down a short hall and into the parlor. It had a bay window looking on the street, an upholstered couch and big chair facing the window. Near it were other soft chairs and two small tables with magazines and books on them.

'Won't you sit down on the sofa, Mr Tretter,' Becky said.

He sank down just before his knees collapsed. His tongue seemed wrapped around his nose. He knew he couldn't say a word if his life depended on it. At last Becky smiled and nodded.

'It's all right. You don't have to be nervous. We're going to talk. About anything you want to. The library, about farrier work, about where you used to live. I want to learn everything about you that I can. First, you said you were eighteen.'

He nodded. 'Be nineteen in August.'

'That's marvelous. You are just six months older than I am.'

He had spoken. He was pleased. Yes, he felt better. Now he saw Mrs Lewton wearing her go-to-meeting dress sitting at a chair across the room. Her back was to them and she had a book in her hands, but he never saw her turn a page. He could do this.

'Only six months? We're almost twins.'

'What about your parents?'

'I lost them in the war.'

'I'm sorry.'

'It was almost five years ago by now.' He shifted on the soft sofa. 'Have you always lived here in East Bend?'

'Oh, no. We've lived here for about five years now. We came from some place in Illinois, but I forget the name of the little town. Father was a doctor there, too, but he wanted to move out West. This is as far as we came. There was no doctor here, so we stopped for a month or so to take care of the people. We just kind of stayed here.'

They went on talking. Both learned a lot about the other person. She told him about going to Normal School where she trained to be a teacher. She had been seventeen when she signed up. Now she taught school with Mrs Benoit. They had only thirty students.

'Most of the boys quit school when they get to be fourteen,' Becky said. 'It's so sad. They should stay in school so they could get better jobs and be better citizens.'

At half past eight, Mrs Lewton cleared her throat and Becky stood. Wade popped up beside her, then stepped back.

'Well, I guess it's time I was leaving,' Wade said. 'It has been a real pleasure talking with you, Miss Rebecca. I look forward to next Sunday.' He almost stumbled as he rushed to the door. He didn't look at Mrs Lewton and she concentrated on her book. At the door Becky shook his hand.

'See you next Sunday,' she said.

Wade nodded and saw her father over her shoulder staring at him. He escaped through the door, down the steps, and past the picket fence.

Once away from the house he tried to relax. He still felt all tied up in knots. He wasn't sure why. The talk had gone well. Not once did Mrs Lewton have to come over and correct them. Yes, it was good. He felt better. He almost ran the rest of the way to the boarding house. It was an hour past 7.30, but he hoped there was still a sandwich or two. He was as hungry as a lonesome coyote with three legs.

Mrs Nelson heard him come in and called.

'Still a sandwich left, Mr Tretter. Be a shame to throw them out.'

He went into the dining room and found three large sandwiches and a pitcher full of cold milk. He sat and took a sandwich. She poured him a glass of milk.

'How did the courting go? she asked. He looked up, surprised. 'Oh, yes. Everyone in town knows about it. Most are pleased. She's a nice girl. Schoolmarm, the doctor's daughter, and educated.' She watched him closely. 'Have another sandwich.'

Later, up in his room, Wade lit the coal-oil lamp and trimmed down the wick. He set it on top of the dresser and looked over the list he'd written out last night.

In the morning, early, he was going

to spoil Rudy Anderson's day. He needed some threat to spring on the man right after he'd convinced him that he had watched the four men murder his parents.

He had it. He'd let Anderson know what happened to Larch Creighton and Bert Daniels. That would give the merchant just a whole potful of problems to think about. Yeah. Wait until tomorrow.

13

Even though it was Sunday, John Brewer was hard at work in his print shop. The door-blind was down, the CLOSED sign hung out, and the front of the shop was dark. Behind the partition three lamps blazed out their light as he and Delbert Greggory worked over the new press that had survived the eighty-mile wagon trip from the railroad up in Nebraska. Greggory had off-loaded it on to the wagon and with an expert teamster brought the heavy press to town.

'At least we have the shipping frame off the press,' Greggory said. The wooden frame had been nailed securely in place. Now the press sat on the slat platform that had supported it.

'Do we need to move it?' Brewer asked. 'Why can't we work with it right there on those wooden planks?'

'Because it has to be on a solid foundation. This old plank floor might even have to be replaced. Just depends how strong the floor is. That press weighs a ton. I'll go to the saloon and hire two strong men to come and help us tip it to the side so we can pound out half of the platform. Then we tip it the other way and pull out the last of the boards.'

'Do it,' Brewer said. He reached into his pocket and pulled out a wad of greenbacks. 'Offer them two dollars each for the work. They'll jump at it.'

An hour later the press was firmly planted on the plank floor which proved to be strong enough to hold it. Greggory fussed around the machine, adjusting levers and checking the ink reservoir and the way the platen moved when he pushed the handle.

After a half-hour of tinkering with the machine he pronounced it fit for duty.

'You bring the paper and the ink?'

'Sure did. Do I look like a tenderfoot

at this business?'

'Sorry, I've been out here in the wilderness for six months. A man forgets.'

'Better not forget anything or there'll be big trouble. We've got to produce. It's my head as well as yours, otherwise neither of us ever goes back to Chicago. Big Bill Jaroose will make certain of that.'

Greggory dug out the precious plates and fitted one on the press, aligned it, then got out the ink and poured a measured amount into the ink well and checked the feeders. He pushed the rollers over the ink feeders and evened out the flow, then tested them. When he was ready he put a piece of paper on the press and pushed the lever. The roller inked the engraving, the platen pressed down hard on the six-by-ten-inch piece of paper, then continued the cycle and swung up from the paper.

Both men leaned in and looked at the print.

'Just about perfect,' Brewer cried out, his face wreathed in smiles, and his fist pounding into the air.

Greggory looked again. 'Not perfect. Ink isn't even. Going to take some work to get everything just right. We'll use scrap paper until it does work perfectly.'

'Looks perfect to me,' Brewer said.

'That's because you don't know what to look for,' Greggory said. 'You'll learn and learn fast, otherwise I have to do all the press work, and a man gets tired after ten to twelve hours on this beast.'

'When will we be ready?' Brewer asked.

'Depends how good you are. Even a thousand will mean two thousand strokes with the press. Takes time. And it has to be perfect every time. Alignment is critical on the second side. So we work at it. If it was simple, lots more people would be doing it.'

* * *

Monday morning when Rudy Anderson opened his mercantile there were two customers waiting at the front door. Ben needed more ten-penny nails. Warren was working on a drain for a first floor bathtub at the hotel. Rudy enjoyed the problem-solving aspect to his business. It wasn't always just taking money for merchandise.

His third customer was the farrier, known to him only as Wade.

'Morning, Wade. You need some more horsehoes?'

'No, Anderson, I don't. You and me need to have a talk.'

'That so. What about.'

'Missouri.'

'Missouri, never been there in my life. Come from Tennessee originally.'

'Oh, you've been in Missouri, Anderson. Last time I saw you there you wore a full Rebel uniform and a cowboy hat. Bring back any memories.'

Anderson looked up quickly, frowned for a moment and his eyes closed down a little. He shifted where he stood and shook his head. 'Don't know what you're talking about. I've got things to do.'

'None more important than our talk.' Wade drew his Colt and leveled it at the merchant.

'Now see here, that's dangerous. That thing could go off. You're no gunman. Take it easy.'

'So you have been in Missouri?'

'Never in my life.'

'I know two men who swore that you were. One was named Bert Daniels. In Missouri he wore a brown scruffy beard. Had his left arm shot up and you wouldn't let a doctor look at it, so after it healed he never could straighten it out. Now do you remember?'

A nervous tic tugged at Anderson's right cheek. He looked around for a moment, his eyes shifting. 'Look, if you're talking about the war, I was a soldier in the Confederate army. I won't deny that. We were mostly around Tennessee and some times fighting up into the Virginias.'

'Another lie, Anderson. Remember

Larch Creighton, the fourth man in your Rebel raiding party, who only had one hand?'

Anderson's face clouded. His glance darted to the counter, then back at the gun already aimed at his belly.

'That six-gun under there won't help much now, Anderson. Remember how the three of you threw Creighton out because he would be too easy to identify? Remember that? You took his share of the money and abandoned him. He became one of the fastest gunmen in eastern Kansas. He killed at least twenty men in shootouts. Finally he came up against one man who got the drop on him and he tried to charge into a pointed and cocked Colt. He's dead now. Dead but never buried.'

Anderson shook his head. 'I don't know those two men so what does all of this have to do with me, Wade?'

'You don't remember a small farm in Missouri? The four of you rode in and my pa came out of the house and said he was a farrier and would shoe your horses free of charge. Without a word all four of you shot him dead where he stood. Then you went into the house and frightened my mother. Daniels went inside looking for guns and he got mad at my mother's name-calling and he killed her with his knife. Now do you remember, you murdering owlhoot?'

'See here. That was a long time ago. We were soldiers — '

'You were rabble, you were deserters, you were freebooters, you were Rebel Raiders and you robbed and killed anyone you found who couldn't defend themselves.'

'We were soldiers — '

'And Captain John Brewer was a soldier too?'

Anderson's head snapped up at Brewer's name.

'Yes, I know he's here in town. A lawyer, and a killer; he's on my list, too. Oh, Daniels is dead. I met him upstate a ways and he caught a .44 slug right through his forehead. He went out with four slugs in his body and begging for mercy. He got a lot more mercy than he showed my ma. So, two down, two to go. You have any preference how you die, Anderson?'

'How you know all this? Them other guys talked?'

Wade told him about the warning and hiding in the grass. 'So I saw you kill my pa, all four of you, and heard your man kill my ma. I become the jury and the executioner.'

Anderson slumped. He shook his head. 'We were just kids, and the war and all . . . ' He looked up at Wade. 'Look, I'll do anything you say. I don't want to die. I've got a wife and two kids — '

'I know about your family. One small problem. If you even think about trying to gun me down, and you miss, I'll come after you and your wife and your kids and put you all in six-foot-deep graves. You understand me?'

'Yes, yes I do.' His eyes flared wide open. For the first time he looked truly terrified. Sweat popped out on his forehead and he slashed at it with his hand.

'Brewer. Don't tell him that I'm in town and know who he is. If he knows, then you're a dead man within twenty-four hours. I'll give you some time to suggest to me how you can make it up to me for killing my parents. You've got two days. Come up with something good. Now, do we understand each other, Anderson, you cowardly, snake in the grass murderer of women and children?'

'Yes. For God's sakes. Just don't hurt my family. I'll do anything you say.'

'You better, Anderson. How many people did you kill during your raiding days?'

He shook his head. 'Don't know. I didn't like that part of it.'

'But you didn't stop it. You were the first to shoot my pa.' Wade lifted the six-gun and aimed it at Anderson's head. 'Let's get this over with right now.' He cocked the weapon and Anderson's face turned chalky white.

'No, I'll work out something. No, for God's sakes, don't shoot.'

A bell sounded on the front door as a customer came in. Wade eased the hammer down from cock and put the Colt back in leather.

'Two days,' he said. He turned his back on the killer and walked out the front door. He adjusted his six-gun in the holster. He would be wearing it from now on wherever he went, except to breakfast, supper, church, and courting. He thought over his talk with Anderson. Surprise, then fear and abject terror had been the progress of his understanding. The threat to his family had been the clincher. He didn't expect any kill try from Anderson.

He walked with a new confidence to the livery stable; found one customer who needed one new shoe put on and had it with him. Wade did the work on the hoof, nailed on the shoe and took the fifty cents the man paid him. Then he went and had a talk with Betsy as he fed her oats and curried her coat. She was getting fatter now that she wasn't working so hard.

He washed up in the watering trough and used a towel that Old Gus had provided for him. Wade combed his hair and then went to see if the library was open. On the way he wondered what solution Anderson would come up with to save his neck. It would be interesting. That aside, he had to decide what his next blow would be against Anderson.

When he went in the library, Becky smiled and waved at him, then talked to a woman at the desk. She wanted a book that Becky didn't have but wound up taking out another one. When she left, Becky motioned for him to come to the small back room shut off from the front by a beaded curtain.

'Father says that you can't come here to the library any more.'

'Why not?'

'Because we're not chaperoned here.'

'Then bring your mother along.'

'She won't come. I've tried to get her to.' Becky reached out and caught his hand, pulled him close to her, then she reached up and kissed his lips. She held the kiss then slowly eased away.

'Mother thinks we might do that.'

'Again,' he said.

They kissed once more and Wade knew that he'd never felt anything like it before. He tried to kiss her again. She smiled, slipped away from him, held his hand, and led him back to the front.

'So, you can't come in unless Mother is here. Check by from time to time and hope. I'm going to appeal to her, one woman to another. In a week's time I think I can persuade her. Now scoot out the door and remember those sweet kisses. I certainly will.' She smiled again and he wanted to grab her, but a woman and an older man came in the door. He smiled and walked out.

On the way back to the boarding house he decided what he had to do next. Insurance. He needed something to help forestall any try on his life. In his room he took out a pair of new lead pencils and his large pad and began writing. He put down the details about the massacre at the farm in Missouri, how he identified the men, and put down the names and descriptions of each one. He wrote down that two of the men were dead. One a famous gunman called One Hand. He made it clear that his parents' murders were not an isolated crime but that this band had been pillaging and killing for perhaps as long as a year just before the war ended. He wrote that he had spoken to Anderson, and if anything happened to him Anderson would be the one responsible for yet another killing. He named John Brewer as the last of the four men and indicated that as of this date although he had exchanged a few words with Brewer he had not mentioned the killings in Missouri, nor had he told Brewer

He sealed the four pages of handwritten message in an envelope and took it to the sheriff's office. On the outside of the envelope he wrote: *28th day of May, 1869. In case of my death, this document is to be opened by the sheriff of East Bend County and action taken.*

Wade had not met Sheriff Engleright. The lawman was about fifty, looked fit, wore scuffed cowboy boots, jeans, and a Western shirt. His face was browned by the wind and sun. He read the message on the outside of the envelope and scowled.

'Somebody aiming you harm, boy?'

'It could happen. I just want some insurance in case it does.'

'This have to do with the war?'

'It does.'

'That's a shame. Wish folks would just leave it be.' He sighed. 'All right. I'll put this in my personal safe. Nobody gets in there but me. If your body turns up somewhere, sometime, I'll dig this out and see what you have to say.'

He thanked the lawman and went back to the livery stable. No business for him. He saddled Betsy and took her on a two-mile jaunt around the back county east of town. She seemed to enjoy the outing. Back at the stable he gave her some oats and put her back in the close lot. She hadn't been rented out yet. Not much call for rentals right now.

He went to the Silent saloon and found a nickel-limit poker game. He bought two dollars' worth of nickels and played for two hours. At the end of that time he counted up his stack of nickels and found that he had lost thirty cents. Wade shrugged. He never had been a good poker player.

He was early for supper that night and talked with the other three men. It had been just another day for them. Wade grinned. It had been a rather full day for him. He had kissed Becky twice and had his confrontation with Anderson. Now all he had to do was decide his next move against the merchant. He had given Anderson two days to come up with some way of compensating him.

That evening after supper he lit the lamp in his room and turned it to a medium flame. Then he slipped out of the house by the back door and made sure that no one followed him. He went by the alley to the low-priced Cattleman's Hotel on Main Street. He waited in the darkness of the alley for ten minutes. When he was sure no one had followed him he went inside, checked in under the name of John Wade and took a room on the first floor. He didn't light a lamp, just lay down on the bed. He tried to sleep but he couldn't get out of his mind the terrified way Anderson had looked at him. The man was still a killer capable of anything. He might take the risk of killing his tormentor.

He had shaken Anderson to his very core. He was not the kind of man to take such a beating and not react. He would react with a vengeance and probably tonight. Wade was alive so far but everyone in town knew where he lived and even which room. It might be a silent killer with a six-gun or a shotgun. He would find out in the morning. It took him a long time to go to sleep.

The ringing bell of the fire engine roused him sometime during the night. He had slept with his clothes on. The old hand-pumper raced down Main Street and charged west. That was toward the Widow Nelson's boarding house. He strapped on his six-gun and hurried out the hotel side door and ran toward the Nelson house. It couldn't be a fire. Nobody would risk the lives of five people to kill one. Nobody? Rudy Anderson just might. He ran faster.

14

A block away from the hotel Wade rounded the corner and saw the Nelson house. No fire. The pumper and its pair of fire horses stood outside the place and six volunteer firemen ran around with nothing to do. When he got closer he saw a thin stream of smoke coming out the second floor window. His window.

He rushed up and found Mrs Nelson standing outside shaking with anger. Somebody brought out a chair for her to sit in. She kicked it over and swore like a teamster.

'Who threw that bomb in my window? Get the polecat, whoever he was, and string him up by his thumbs. I want that galoot dead by noon.'

The sheriff ran up and looked at the situation. Somebody pointed out Mrs Nelson and he talked with her.

'So you heard an explosion and it nearly threw you out of bed. By the time you got upstairs the curtains were on fire and you tore them down and stomped them out. Anybody in that room?'

'Supposed to be. Rented it to that farrier man, Mr Tretter. But he warn't anywhere around I could see. Unless he was buried under the mattress which was torn all to pieces. I swear, Sheriff, I want you to find this bomber and you let me drag him through the brush land for a few miles in back of a good horse.'

'Yes, Mrs Nelson. We'll do our best. Why don't you show me the room?'

Mrs Nelson turned and saw Wade. She ran to him and threw her arms around him.

'Thank God you're safe, young man. I was so worried. Come with us; let's see if it ruined all your things.'

Upstairs they used two lamps to inspect the damage. Wade looked at his pocket watch. It was 3.30 a.m. Good time for a bombing, nobody around.

The room was shattered inside. The dresser was on its side and the bowl and pitcher lay broken on the floor. The curtains were black with soot and ashes. The bed had been blown apart. He guessed the bomb had landed on the bed before it went off. The blankets and sheets were shredded and the mattress was scattered in a dozen pieces around the room. The window glass was spread all over. Only now was the smell of the explosion blowing out through the window. The dresser drawers had come open but by then the blast was over and most of his clothes were intact. His saddle in the far corner had sustained little damage. His Farmer's Pride flour sack with his camping goods in it was ripped apart.

'Looks like you're lucky to be alive, Mr Tretter,' the sheriff said. He scowled. 'You gave me that letter this afternoon. You have any idea something like this . . . ?'

Wade shook his head. 'There was a chance, but I didn't think anything would happen so fast.' He set up the dresser and pushed the drawers back in place. The other boarders crowded in the hallway looking inside. They offered to help put things right.

Wade shook his head. 'Best get back to sleep, you men. You have to go to work tomorrow. Looks like I have the day off.'

The sheriff shook his head. 'Don't know why folks do this kind of thing. Looks like I have enough to write up a report. First time we've had a house bombing since I've been here. I'll check the mercantile first thing in the morning to find out if anyone has bought two or three sticks of dynamite lately. You think two sticks did it?'

'I'd say two, Sheriff. Three might have caved in the wall and blown a hole in the roof.' The sheriff waved and went out of the room and down to the yard. He told the firemen to take the volunteer rig back to the firehouse.

Wade and Mrs Nelson set about getting the room in order. The brass bedframe and head- and footboards were intact. The mattress they carried out in pieces and put in a burn barrel in the back yard. The bedboards had been blown off their fittings and the springs now slumped on the floor.

'Got me a spare mattress out in the shed by the barn in back,' Mrs Nelson said. 'We can bring it up in the morning.' She put her hands on her hips. 'The sidewinder. Any idea who might want you hurt bad or even dead, Mr Tretter?'

'A couple, but I'm not going to give any names yet.' He was thinking about Anderson. The man still had a Rebel raider heart. Wade knew he should go down town and burn down the mercantile. Even up the score just a bit. But he remembered his pledge to himself not to do any thing to Anderson that would harm the family.

It was after 4.30 by the time they had the glass all swept up and the burned curtains gathered up and hauled away. Wade righted the wooden chair, which looked undamaged, and sat down. It had been a wild day and night for him.

Mrs Nelson set her fists on her hips and glowered at the room.

'About all we can do now,' she said. 'You can catch a nap on the couch downstairs. I'll get you a pillow and a blanket.'

He protested but she wouldn't listen. She provided the goods, he took off his boots, and curled up on the couch.

The next thing he knew he heard the boarders chattering in the dining room. He lifted up, slipped into his boots, and finger-combed his hair before he hurried into the next room.

'The ghost,' one man said.

'The guy who almost was dead,' another said.

He waved at them, took his place, dished out a big bowl of oatmeal, then had two eggs, bacon, toast, and coffee.

'Glad the little problem last night didn't affect your appetite, Mr Tretter,' the widow said, and they all chuckled.

After breakfast one of the boarders

helped Wade with the mattress, lugging it up the stairs to the bed. They set the bedboards in the rails along the side, then swung the springs on the boards and put the mattress on top of that. Mrs Nelson took over and made up the bed with sheets, one blanket, and a new pillow.

Both panes of the double-hung windows had been blown out by the blast. They found glass outside as well as in, so the bomb must have crashed through one window as it went inside and the blast blew the other one all over the front yard.

'Panes of glass that big gonna take a while to get here,' Mrs Nelson said. 'The mercantile has to order them special. I'll go down and put in an order. Till then, I'll hang a heavy blanket over the window, if that'll be all right?'

'Fine, Mrs Nelson. Now I better check in at the livery, see if I can earn my week's board-and-room money.'

There was one customer waiting for

him. The mount needed three new shoes. He sent the man up to the mercantile to buy the shoes. Then he put them on and collected his dollar and a half.

Old Gus was curious. 'Hear you almost got yourself blown to bits last night.'

'Not even close. I wasn't in the room at the time. Had a feeling somebody might try to harm my bones.'

'You figure out who?'

'Yep. But I don't want him dead just yet.'

'Be careful, boy. Our sheriff might look kind of slow but he's sharp as a new-filed hoe.'

'I'll be careful.'

'Notice that you're wearing your Colt.'

'About time.' Wade put his farrier tools away and headed up to Main Street. He had a call to make.

He slipped up the alley and found the back door to the mercantile. It even had a sign on it. The door was unlocked, so he edged it open, saw no one on the back room, and stepped inside. He was going to surprise Rudy Anderson and maybe scare him out of the rest of his life.

Wade stood behind a stack of cardboard boxes, watching the front of the store through the door. He saw Anderson moving around, waiting on customers. Wade worked closer to the door. Anderson came into the back room quickly after something. Wade dropped behind some stacks of goods and waited. The merchant went out front a moment later and gave the product to the customer.

When Wade heard the doorbell ring again he figured the last customer had left the store and he edged up to the door. Anderson stood behind the small counter evidently going through his cash box. Wade drew his Colt and fired a round into the wooden floor a foot from Anderson's feet. Anderson bel-lowed in surprise and rage, jumped back a step, then turned toward where he had heard the sound.

'I'm a ghost, Anderson. You killed me last night with that bomb, now I'm back to haunt you for the rest of your life.'

Anderson sagged against the counter.

'Tretter, you damn near scared me to death. I don't know who did that last night. Wasn't me and Brewer don't know who you are or what you know.'

'Liar, Anderson. I should kill one of your kids tonight just to get even with you. You get one more chance. What have you come up with to keep me from killing you?'

'I've got a plan. Good one. We go into partnership in the mercantile here. I sign over forty-nine per cent of the store to you for one dollar to make it a legal and binding bill of sale. You and I split the profits, but I have control of the store. You don't have to lift a finger, or even stay in town. I'm making from a hundred and fifty to two hundred dollars of profit a month from the store. That's as much as most men make in a whole year. Good deal. Honest. Then you leave me and my family alone. You don't threaten us, you don't tell my wife about any of this.'

Anderson stared at Wade. The merchant wiped his forehead, then cleared his throat three times. He looked around from place to place and put his hands in his pockets, then he took them out.

Let him sweat, Wade decided.

After a minute of no response from Wade, Anderson spoke again. 'So what do you say? It's a terrible financial loss to me, but I can stand it if you leave my family alone.'

'Sounds interesting. First, move away from your weapon under the counter.' Anderson did. Wade holstered his gun. A customer came in and Wade nodded at the storeman to wait on him. The customer needed a new horse-collar. There were two sizes and he took the larger one. He paid for it and left. Anderson turned to Wade again.

'How can you prove to me that you

didn't throw that bomb last night or hire someone to do the job?'

'You know I can't. Can you prove that you didn't throw that bomb yourself? Of course not. It's impossible to prove a negative. The only way is to find the person who did it. That will be hard.'

'I'm warning you that I left a letter with the sheriff, to be opened if I turn up dead. It tells the facts about you four in Missouri and your crimes. If you do manage to kill me, your name will be mud in this town and you'll wind up in prison. So think that through.'

Anderson shook his head. 'Wasn't me. Won't be me. You want this deal on the store or not? You guarantee to leave me and my family alone and you get forty-nine per cent of the store and half of the profits. I've got the paper all written out. All you have to do is sign it and I sign it and we both have a copy.'

'I'll think about it. First I want you to donate a hundred dollars to the East Bend public library, so they can buy new books. Take the money down there today.'

'Or else?'

'Or else I'll shoot you dead before midnight.'

Anderson closed his eyes a ways and stared at the younger man. At last he shrugged. 'I think you'd do it. All right. A hundred dollars to the library today. You'll do well to accept my offer for half the store. I might not make it again.'

'You will. You want to live. Don't tell anyone why you're giving the library the money.'

Wade turned his back on the merchant and walked out the front door. He had no fear that the killer would shoot him in the back.

* * *

Greggory compared his print with the sample he was trying to duplicate. He had it almost right. A little bit more correction in the ink flow and he'd have it. He made the adjustment, then he did two test runs, then he put the special paper on the press and made the print. He lifted it off the press and held it up a moment to dry, then lay it face up on the table with the lamp close by.

Brewer rushed over to see it. The older man looked at the printer, who grinned. 'Yes, this time, we've got it. Perfect. Even a judge himself couldn't tell the difference. Feast your eyes, Mr Brewer, soon to be a rich man because of a thousand perfect counterfeited United States ten-dollar notes.'

'Amazing, just like in Chicago. How many do we make on the first run?'

'A thousand is what we figured. That means two thousand strokes of the press. We run the front of the bills first, then take that plate out and run them through with them perfectly aligned with the engraving for the back of the bills. A little tricky, but with this press we can come out right ninety-nine times out of a hundred.'

'My God, a thousand ten dollar bills

is ten thousand dollars.'

Greggory turned to face his partner. 'One thing straight and true right now. None of these bills, not even one, gets passed here in town or anywhere near East Bend. That's a must. We don't want anyone sniffing around our printing plant.'

'Oh, absolutely, Greggory. I know that. The first five hundred bills we finish we send by registered mail to our friend in Chicago. The next five hundred we pass them ourselves. If we can average eight dollars in change each time we pass one bill, we should be able to come home with four thousand dollars in honest, bona fide greenbacks.'

'Yeah, but a lot of work to do before that day. Now leave me alone and let me do a couple hundred before noon. I'm going to be starved. You have enough real money to buy me a steak dinner?'

'I can manage that. How far away do we have to go before we start passing the bills?'

Greggory put a new sheet of the good paper on the press and turned. 'At least fifty miles. We'll ride horses to the nearest stageline stop and go from there. That's the tricky part. We have to turn into actors and be able to change our appearance. The bills will be spotted, and when they are, the federal folks will try like crazy to track us down by questioning the merchants who took in the bills.'

'Yeah. I can't wait. Quit talking and get printing. All this talk about money is making me hungry.'

15

At supper that night, Mrs Nelson made an announcement.

'This is mostly for Mr Tretter. Often on Tuesday nights we have a domino game here on the big table. We use double twelves and play on all doubles. To make it interesting we play for a penny a point. We add up the ends of all the ends and only multiples of five count: five, ten, fifteen, forty-five. Game goes to five hundred points. First person who gets five hundred collects a penny a point from each player who has less.' She looked at Wade. 'Want to play?'

'Why not, get some fresh money in the game.' The others cheered. As soon as the dinner dishes were cleared and washed, and the kitchen cleaned up, Mrs Nelson brought out the dominoes. A double five by Wade started the game, scoring Wade ten points.

'I think I like this game already,' he said. The play settled down. He quickly saw the strategy: make all the points you can.

Joe Welton, the saddle-maker, was quick and sure. He could count up the ends of the lines of dominoes faster than anyone. Mike Swensen, the barber was slower, but built up points fast. Mrs Nelson seemed to be just happy to play and wasn't concerned about points. Ken Vincent, the clerk, played hard but missed chances to score.

The first game ended when Welton reached 500 points. Wade had 312. He owed the saddle-maker a dollar and eighty-eight cents. This was more expensive than nickel poker down at the saloon.

He played one more game and won it, taking in over three dollars and came out a dollar ahead. He wandered out of the house and headed for a poker game. He liked the challenge of a good five-card-draw game and there usually was one around. But he would keep it to the nickel-a-bet variety. He was halfway to the saloon when a shadow stepped out of a dark alley and fired three pistol shots at him from thirty feet. They missed.

Wade drew and fired once, ran into the alley, and saw the man staggering down the passage way. A splash of light from the saloon's rear windows outlined him. He was wounded. Wade raced toward him. He had to find out who he was and who had hired him. Before he got there a door opened six feet from the shooter and three more pistol shots thundered in the alley. The bushwhacker stumbled and dove head first into the garbage-littered alley.

The bushwhacker was dead. Wade figured it by the way the man fell and didn't move. The person who killed him was in the saloon. Wade raced out of the alley and for the saloon's front door. No one came out. He stepped inside and watched the men at the tables and the bar. A man stood to go out the back door, evidently to the outhouse. No one came in from that direction. Wade saw no one in the saloon whom he knew. Certainly Rudy Anderson wasn't there. He bought a beer at the bar and went back to the nickel-poker table. He had played with two of the men before. They made room for him as the fifth at the table. He slid into the chair, bought two dollars' worth of coins, and settled in to play. He lost steadily. Sometimes he forgot what cards he held. Instead he watched the faces in the saloon and at the tables. He wanted to recognize them if he saw them again. Somewhere in the crowd of about thirty men had to be the shooter who killed the bush-whacker. Or was he? The same man could have heard Wade running for the front of the saloon, then stepped out into the alley, and vanished in the night. Who was he?

Wade quit the game when he lost the two dollars. He was down a dollar for the night. He gave it up and walked to the front door. He stepped outside, then came back in quickly to see if anyone had moved to the door to follow him. Nobody had. He went outside again and hurried through the darkness, keeping to the buildings so he wouldn't make himself a target. He made it to the boarding house, went in the back door as he had told Mrs Nelson he was going to do, and up to his room. He didn't bother with a lamp. Instead he took off his boots, slid out of his pants and dropped on the bed. The room still smelled of the dynamite. He'd get used to it in a rush.

* * *

Wednesday morning after breakfast he walked past the library. He paused in front of the window. Becky looked up and saw him. She hurried to the door.

'Hi, nice suitor-type gentleman Mr Wade Tretter.'

'Good morning. Is this legal? I'm not in the library.'

'Sounds fair to me. The most wonderful thing happened yesterday afternoon. That nice Mayor Anderson came by and gave us a hundred dollars to use to buy books. Mrs Young, she's the librarian you haven't met, has all sorts of publishers' catalogs and she's working over them. She said she should be able to get a lot of new books for under a dollar each. That could be a hundred new books.'

'That's great news. Good for the library. I'd guess your mother isn't inside?'

'No, sorry. I'm working on her.'

'Good. I've got to get down to the livery. I'll try to stop by on the boardwalk again this afternoon.' He touched her shoulder a moment and felt her shiver, then pulled away, and walked toward the mercantile.

Anderson saw him come in and headed for the counter.

'Don't go back there, Anderson. We need to talk. You tried again last night. You missed again. Only you had to hire two killers this time. One of your men dead in the alley, the other one hiding in the saloon.'

'Don't know what you're talking about.'

'Right you don't know. That's what I told your wife this morning. She didn't understand. I swear that I didn't mean to hurt her in any way. Things just got out of hand.'

Anderson's face clouded and he exploded in a rage. 'My wife! You went to see my wife? If you so much as touched her I'll run you down like the scum you are.' He ran to the front of the store, put out the closed sign and waited for Wade to saunter out the door. Then he slammed it and ran down the street toward his house.

Wade grinned and headed for the livery. He hadn't gone to see Mrs Anderson. But he'd put the fear of the devil in Anderson when he suggested that he had. A little bit of getting even.

When Wade got to the livery he had two cowboys with mounts that needed hoof work. A towner came in with his mare and before noon Wade had pocketed six dollars.

Old Gus laughed and shook his head. 'By damn, but you are good with that hammer and chisel. I never got the hang of it. Pleasure to watch you work.'

'I should sell tickets.'

'Wouldn't go that far. You know who tried to blow you up?'

'Yep.'

'You gonna even the score?'

'Want to, but he's got a wife and two kids. I blow him into dirt city, who is going to take care of his family?'

'Yeah, there's that.' They sat there watching the wind whip up little dust devils and prance them across the street.

'This gent have any kin? They could take in the family.'

Wade brightened. He sat up from the bench. 'Yeah, never thought of that. I'll ask around. Makes the whole day seem better. Find me some more shoeing business.' He headed up town. He needed to talk with Becky. She was the only one he could trust.

There were four children in the library when Wade looked in the window. He waited until they found books and left. He tapped on the glass. Becky saw him, smiled, and hurried to the door.

'Come in, I want you to meet my mother.'

'She's here?'

'Yes, she has decided she likes you and wants to help us. Come inside.'

In the room with its stacks of books he saw Mrs Nelson sitting in a chair near the far wall. They went over to her and she looked up.

'Mother, I'd like you to meet my friend, Wade Tretter.'

'Ma'am,' Wade said, bobbing his head. She looked up, her face neutral, then a small smile broke through. She held out her hand encased in a white glove. He took it carefully.

'Young man, Mr Wade Tretter. I've decided that I like you and I don't want my husband to scare you off. I'll be here three days a week in the afternoons until about three. Monday, Wednesday and Friday. Be a good time for you and Becky to work on the library shelves and books. She tells me you're good with a hammer and nails.'

'Mrs Lewton, it's good to meet you. I try with the hammer. My father was a real carpenter. I'm so pleased that you came here.'

She frowned. 'The very idea that two young people can get to know each other in two hours a week is ridiculous. Men make up the rules. But sometimes we get to bend them a little. He said you can't see Becky unless you're chaperoned. I agreed. Well I'm here and I'm your chaperone. Now get on with your business. Must be some books to be marked or shelved or something. I'm busy reading a novel by Louisa May Alcott. I try to read everything she writes. Go along now.'

They went over by the shelves. 'Isn't she wonderful?' Becky said.

'Almost as wonderful as her only daughter.' They looked at each other and he thought that he'd never been happier. She lifted her brows.

'Now, Mr Tretter, it's time you met our librarian, Mrs Young. She's been out when you've been here before. She has a little office in back. Come on.' They went through another door into the large rear area of the old retail store and to an office built at one side. Becky opened the door and they looked in. A woman in her thirties sat at a desk with half a dozen book publishers' catalogs spread out in front of her. She looked up.

'Mrs Young, this is Wade Tretter whom I've told you about. He's made most of our bookshelves and is a big help.'

She stood and was nearly as tall as Wade, and thin. She held out a hand. Her smile was genuine and warm. 'Glad to meet you. Becky here talks of nothing else.' She nodded. 'I think she's right. Thanks for the help on the bookshelves. I flunked carpenter's school. A hammer to me is a tool to use to smash your own thumb.' They all laughed.

'We'll let you spend all that money,' Becky said.

Mrs Young waved at the catalogs. 'These are interesting to look at, but when I have to decide which books to buy, it turns into work.'

They talked a little more, then Becky and Wade went back into the library. No one had come in while they were gone. Becky motioned to the far side of the room.

'Wade, there is one more bookcase that we need to finish, and I'm not sure we should put books on the top shelf. No one can reach them except you unless we furnish a step-stool.'

They worked for an hour on the bookcase, then Wade found a spot to get in his question.

'What about this new mayor? Will he appoint all of his family and friends to all the city jobs?'

Becky shook her head and he watched her hair bounce. 'Don't think he'll do that. He married one of the North girls. There are just two of them and the other sister still lives at home.'

No chance there for the in-laws to take in a daughter and two more kids. That was not a help.

'I guess there aren't many city jobs to worry about, anyway. Do you want me to finish that next bookcase?'

They worked until three, then Mrs Lewton found them getting the shelving put in place.

She smiled at Wade. 'Young man, it's been good meeting you this way. Today must still be Wednesday. I'll be back here at the library Friday at one o'clock. I'll look for you here.' She nodded at them and went out the door. Wade pressed Becky's hand, gave her a quick hug and hurried out the door just behind Mrs Lewton.

Wade got in the first words. 'Mrs Lewton, thank you for coming and for believing in me.'

'It's just what's right. I'll see you again on Friday.' She turned and walked off, striding toward her yellow-trimmed house.

* * *

John Brewer hovered over the man working the press. Twice Greggory had hit him on the shoulder, yelling at him to stand back to give him room to get his work done. Greggory had finished printing the front sides of the thousand counterfeit ten-dollar bills. They were stacked to one side in ten piles of a hundred each. They had not been trimmed yet to the exact size of the federally made currency. He was working on getting the alignment of the new plate to match exactly that of the old one. Then the printing would be perfectly aligned and the front would be in the precise position over the back of the printed bill. It was the most important adjustment that he had to make and it had to be perfect. A hundredth of an inch off and it would show on the finished bills and they would be spotted.

Greggory made one more minor adjustment, locked down the spacers on the press and stared at the engraving. It was one of the best he had ever seen working in this racket for ten years. No one but an expert could tell it from the real ten-dollar greenback. The one element that could trip them up was the serial number on the bill. The numbers on the bills would be exactly the same. He didn't have the web-type press that printed the real bills, which could also be set to increase one number each time a single bill was printed.

He stepped back, gave the press a final look, then put one of the already printed front of the ten-dollar bills, and positioned it precisely on the press. Greggory took a deep breath and pulled the lever to bring the platen down and print the back of the bill on the paper. He opened the press and took out the sheet of paper. He held it up to the pair of coal-oil lamps and studied it.

'So, how is it? Is this whole thing going to work? Tell me, what you think?'

'Perfect,' Greggory said. 'Watch the wet ink but take a look for yourself.'

He handed the printed bill to Brewer holding it carefully by the inch-wide border around it, which would be trimmed off. Brewer looked at the bill, studied the front, then the back, and then held it up to the light. The pair of straight lines around the sides of the bill and the single printed line on top and bottom were registered precisely with the somewhat free form line following the elements of the rear of the bill.

'Perfect,' John Brewer said. He let out a Rebel yell that made Greggory wince.

'Hold down the yelling. We don't want anyone to get curious.'

Brewer looked at the serial number on the front of the bill: K38476838A. So long a number, but then it would be harder for people to remember that number. He mentioned the idea to Greggory.

'Yeah, some will forget it. The problem comes when some merchant or some banker gets two bills and compares the serial numbers. Some bankers do that, trying to get bills in serial order.'

'That could be bad for us,' Brewer said. He slicked back his hair with his right hand.

'Get out of here, Brewer, you make me nervous. I have to do these exactly right, or it costs us eight greenbacks per mistake.'

'Yeah, up to you now. I'll get supper at one of these eateries disguised as restaurants, then head on home. Don't work too late. The later it is the more mistakes you'll make. See you tomorrow.'

16

Wade left the library after a wave to Becky through the window. He had seen more buggies here than in some of the towns. The streets were two inches of powder-fine dust that turned into mud when it rained. The buggies were clumsy-looking affairs with four tall wire-spoked wheels, holding up a frame with a seat for two. They were pulled by a single horse that was hitched to them by iron rings on the front of the frame, which took the traces from the harness of one horse.

He had seen Anderson drive his fancy buggy up to the front of his store and leave it there, sometimes all morning. It was still there today as he walked past the store. He had been beating his brain cells for two days now trying to think of ways he could humiliate Anderson without actually hurting him physically or financially. The buggy kept leaping into his thoughts.

Few of the other merchants drove a buggy to work. Those who did usually left the rigs behind their stores, most unhitching the horses.

Wade had the idea in a flash of laughter. He sauntered past the rig he knew belonged to Anderson. The horse was patiently waiting for time to go home and find its bucket of oats. Wade stopped at the horse's head and patted her, stroked her neck, then worked back to her hindquarters. Yes, the traces, the heavy leather straps that harnessed the horse to the buggy were fastened in two places on the front of the buggy. One on each side. He reached down and unhooked the heavy fasteners of the harness from the buggy on both sides. The horse was now free of the buggy, but would stand where she was until urged to move with a slap of the reins on her back.

Wade drifted into the Kansas Café

and had a cup of coffee as he watched the buggy. He had seen Anderson quitting his store sometimes at 4.30, leaving a clerk in charge until closing time around seven. It was just after half past four.

Wade finished his coffee and went outside where he sat in a captain's chair backed up against the eatery on the almost new boardwalk. He leaned the chair backwards on its rear legs until the back touched the wall, then sat there surveying the town.

Five minutes later Anderson came out of his store, hurried down two stores and stepped up to the seat of the carriage. He untied the reins from the side posts. He said something to the mare, slapped the reins lightly on her back, and the horse stepped ahead. When she felt no strain on the harness she bolted forward. The buggy remained in place as the horse trailing the reins and traces, ran down the street and vanished around the corner of the second block. Anderson sat in the buggy where the reins had been jerked out of his hands staring at the vanishing horse.

'Hey, Anderson, your horse forgot something,' somebody yelled at the merchant.

'Anderson, didn't anybody tell you that you have to hitch the horse to the buggy before it will move?' another voice called. A dozen people gathered on the boardwalk in front of the buggy. Those eyewitnesses told others who came to see what had happened and laughter rippled through the small crowd.

Anderson stepped out of the buggy, trying to regain his dignity, huffed at the crowd, and marched swiftly down the boardwalk in the direction the horse had taken.

Wade laughed with the others. There was no problem with the horse. She would run a ways then walk on to her small stable behind the Andersons' house. Most horses knew the way home if they had been at a ranch or a home stall for more than a few months.

Wade checked his pocket watch and headed for the boarding house. He didn't want to be late for supper. Tonight he had to do some serious thinking about how he could cow and humiliate Rudy Anderson without actually harming him. The harming might come later; he wasn't sure of that yet. He probably should meet or at least get a look at the Anderson family. Since his target was the mayor, Wade was sure he would go to church Sunday. Wade would make it his main task to find the Anderson family and remember who they were at church.

Supper at the boarding house was special that night. A friend of Mrs Nelson had gone hunting that afternoon and brought her two Chinese pheasants. She had roasted both of them in her oven and the men tore into them greedily. Wade had often had pheasant. He considered it twice as tasty as chicken. She had roasted it with some kind of spices and stuffing that was delicious. That, along with the rest of the dishes including boiled potatoes and gravy, baked beans, just baked bread, new peas, fresh-churned butter, and the last of the strawberry jam, made a meal to remember. Wade also downed two cups of coffee.

After supper he went up to his room, lit his lamp and stood at his desk on the top of the dresser, ready to make out a list of how he could get even with Rudy Anderson.

He couldn't find the old list he'd made, so he started a new one on his pad of paper. He began with the worst punishment of all, and went from there putting down anything no matter how wild or strange or gentle. His list:

Shoot him dead.
Run him out of town.
Burn down his mercantile.
Cripple him with shots in both knees so he'd never walk again without crutches.
Humiliate him in every way

possible.
Print his story of pillage and murder in the local newspaper.
Tell his wife about his murderous past so she would divorce him.
Charge him with voter fraud in the election for mayor.
Charge him with attempted murder in the two kill-tries against Wade Tretter.
Spread rumors that he secretly owned the big saloon.
Spread rumors that he was wanted for murder in Missouri.

Wade looked over the list and shook his head. None of the actions seemed right. He still had misgivings about harming the man's wife and children.

He looked over the list again. Nothing seemed right. He wasn't about to shoot the man. The rumors he could start, but they wouldn't hurt him that much. Harassment was an idea. But how? The unhitched buggy had been a good one today. But what else? And how did that do much of anything to settle a score for two murders?

He went to sleep trying to come up with some more ideas. He thought of telling Mrs Nelson the whole story, but at last decided she would have no good ideas for near mayhem and malicious retribution. He guessed that her quick answer to his questions would be to 'shoot the murderer dead.'

Thursday morning he had no customers at the livery, but by ten o'clock a rider came in from the Lazy W cattle ranch fifteen miles north of town. The cowboy was young, tanned, with a worn cowboy hat, and a much-used lariat on his saddle. He wore a blue shirt and a red neckerchief that had seen more than one dust storm. He eased down from his mount, ground-tied her, and waved at Wade.

'You the farrier?'

'Yep. I'm Wade Tretter.' He held out his hand.

'I'm Shorty. We can use you out at the Lazy W. We got twenty riders out there and two of them had you work on their mount hoofs. They say you did a good job. We want you to come out to the ranch and look over our remuda. Getting ready for a round-up and drive to the railhead. We'll have twelve men on the ride with four horses each since it's a short run. Should be about sixty nags for you to check over and work on any in need. You still charge fifty cents a hoof?'

'Usual.'

'You could have over a hundred hoofs to work. If you do more than fifty, we'll pay you thirty-five cents each.'

'Who pays?'

'Each rider pays for his own mount. The boss takes care of the remuda horses.'

Wade figured it quickly. If he did a hundred hoofs that would be thirty-five dollars. More than he would make in two weeks of town work. Besides, he had about caught up most of the town horses, and business was slowing down.

'Give you a bunk and grub for as

long as it takes,' the cowboy said.

'What about new shoes?'

'Langdon bought three kegs of different sizes. He says he figures he has about a hundred shoes. If we bring another fifty each, we should have enough.'

Wade held out his hand. 'Cowboy, you've got yourself a deal.'

Wade sent the cowboy to the mercantile to buy the horseshoes they would need. He went to the boarding house and packed a small valise with two pairs of pants and some shirts, and took a box of .44 rounds for his Colt, which he had been wearing every day lately. He told Mrs Nelson he'd be gone a few days.

Shorty rode back to the livery with word that he could buy only forty shoes from the mercantile.

'Said he had to save a few for folks in town and travelers. Says he can't get any more for two weeks.'

They rode to the mercantile and packed the shoes in their saddle-bags and tied sacksful on the back of their saddles. Then they hit the trail north and west into cattle country.

It took them a little over four hours to travel the distance. When they arrived Shorty led Wade to the cook-house, where the cook worked up a dinner for them. They had steaks, potatoes and gravy, some new-grown green beans, and gallons of coffee. Then Wade went to work.

He did the cowboys' mounts first. Half of the men were on the range. By the time he had done the ten riders working around the ranch, he had done thirty-two hoofs and cleaned up the rest of them. Most of the mounts had overgrown hoofs.

It was dark by the time he finished and the supper bell rang. Wade was so tired he forgot what they had for supper, but he thought it was some kind of stew with big chunky vegetables and apple pie for dessert.

Shorty showed him a bed in the bunkhouse and he dropped on it too tired to do more than say hello to the cowboys who drifted in. A poker game had just started when he dozed off.

Friday morning he began working at daylight and by noon had most of the second bunch of ten riders happy with their mounts. This group had taken better care of the hoofs and he had to replace only eighteen shoes. He collected the thirty-five cents a shoe from each man as he went along and put the cash in a purse he slung on a leather thong around his neck and under his shirt. By noon Saturday he had done fifty shoes. The owner, Mr Langdon, came out and they looked over the remuda at a close-in pasture. The mounts would be used on the trail drive and round-up. That way each rider would have four horses. He would ride a different one each day for four days, then go back to the first one, giving the mounts time to rest up between the tough work of a round-up and the trail drive.

Wade and the ranch owner checked

each mount. Those that needed shoes or hoof work were put into the corral and the others sent to a separate pasture. By the time they had the horses all looked over the supper bell rang. Wade counted fifteen of the horses that would need work, most of them three or four shoes.

It took Wade another day and a half to finish the last of the remuda horses. The owner brought in six more he decided needed hoof work after all. Mr Langdon paid him for the work on the remuda mounts and Wade counted up his bankroll. He had done 107 shoes, and should have made thirty-seven dollars and forty-five cents.

He left about noon on the fourth day, and it wasn't until he was halfway into town that afternoon that he remembered that it had to be Monday. He had missed talking with Mrs Lewton on Friday, missed church Sunday, and missed his courting time with Becky on Sunday evening. He figured that the doctor would understand, but Becky might be a tougher sell. Monday: Mrs Lewton should be at the library from noon to three today. He could tell her and Becky at the same time. No, it was already past two o'clock, he'd be far too late to catch her by three.

He had left the ranch a little after noon and hit town just after five. He washed up and just made it to supper at the boarding house. It was a pork-chop meal. After supper he took a quick bath, put on clean clothes, and hurried over to the Lewton house. He knocked on the front door.

Becky opened the door and stared at him. 'It's you, the missing man. I was worried about you.'

'Is your mother here?' he asked.

Becky's slight frown deepened. 'Yes, and she's worried too. You missed church and then missed our courting time.'

'I can explain.'

Mrs Lewton came out of the living room and watched him a moment. 'I'm sure you can explain,' she said. She went to her favorite chair near the front window and he and Becky followed.

He told them about the job he had at the Lazy W, and that he had made over thirty-five dollars. He explained it all to them and for a moment they were satisfied. Then Becky's frown grew.

'You should have told me that you would be gone.'

'It all happened so fast. I know now that I should have left you a message or something. Sorry. The next time I have to be gone, if there is ever a next time, I'll be sure to let you know.'

Mrs Lewton raised one hand at him and nodded. 'Fine, Mr Tretter. I'll explain your absence to my husband. He'll be glad you made the money. Shows initiative and dependability, he'll say.'

Becky pouted a moment, then recovered. 'We got a whole box of books that a man leaving town donated to the library. Some of them are old. Some even have real leather bindings. A few of them must be worth three or four dollars each, at least. One of them has two of Shakespeare's plays.'

She frowned and put her hands on her hips.

'We do have a problem at the library. We're getting so many books we have to separate them somehow. How can we do this?'

They talked about it and at last decided they should start by separating fiction books from fact. They talked a little more and then Wade said he had to leave. He was glad that he had been able to explain his absences to the satisfaction of Becky and her mother.

Back at the boarding house he went up to his room and looked over his list of ways to get revenge on Rudy Anderson.

He stared at the list and went over and over it. Then he remembered in detail the men riding into the small farm and his father offering to fix their horses' hoofs. He relived the moment when Rudy Anderson had pulled his six-gun and shot his father from six feet away. There was only one way for him to get justice for what Anderson had done to his father.

Rudy Anderson had to die.

17

Delbert Greggory wiped sweat from his forehead with his arm and lifted the last printed ten-dollar bill from the press. He put it on the table beside the others to dry. The ink would be set in two hours but he would need more time than that to trim off the borders of the bills he'd printed during the last four days.

He sat in the chair he had moved in by the press and considered his work. Some of his best. The registration was perfect. If it wasn't he pitched it into the burn barrel and every evening he had a fire in the barrel out in the alley.

He looked at the stacks of bills. The small print-shop had a good blade-trimmer. The sharp cutter was two feet long, eight inches high, and came down in a slantwise motion across the material to be cut, which was held tightly in a press.

With the cutter he could trim off one side of thirty bills at a time. The cut on each side would be different, depending how wide the unprinted paper was. He would cut all the tops of the bills first, then all the bottoms and then both ends winding up with a trimmed beautiful ten-dollar counterfeit bill. He felt a tingle of excitement as he always did when he had just finished a print run. They might be able to pass this bunch for years before the federal treasury people tracked them down.

He started the trimming, estimating the number of bills for each cut. Gradually he increased the number until he had a stack almost an inch thick, which the heavy blade cut through as though it was a ripe melon.

It took him the rest of the day to finish the cutting. Brewer and their silent partner Mayor Anderson had been in and fondled the bills. Anderson was like a small boy in a candy store. Greggory relented and let him take three of the fake bills with him. But he warned him about keeping them safe. Brewer was getting used to them before he started passing them. They would plan out their routes tonight, then tomorrow they would ride out with their supply of bills. He had 500 bills that he would package up and send by registered mail at the first post office he came to serviced by a stageline. Registered mail had been initiated by the post office in 1855. The package would go to their mentor/partner in Chicago, Big Bill Jaroose.

Both he and Brewer would have 250 bills. He would use his to pass on the general route south-east toward Manhattan. He'd pass bills at every small town he stopped at along the way. A larger-sized town meant he might stay two days, working various stores. Then he would head for Topeka, again stopping at every small town, and pass as many bills as he felt was safe. He would continue on as far as Topeka where he would pass as many of the bills as he could. On a good day he should be able to move twenty-five bills. Then he'd go to all of the small towns around that area and pass more of the ten spots. He'd buy an item for under a dollar and get nine good greenbacks in change.

He would head back to East Bend by a different route hitting small towns on the way and passing bills wherever he could. He would keep to the stagecoach routes so he had fast transportation.

Brewer would head due south and slightly east to Concordia where he was sure there would be a stage. From there the stage would go south all the way to Salina, with Brewer hitting every town along the route. After maybe two days in Salina, he would go on south to Wichita, the largest town in that part of the state, where he should be able to pass a lot of paper. When he'd finished there he would come back north. He would not be able to pass any of the bills on the way back since there was only one stage route that went north over in that sparsely populated area. He had worked the towns on the way down.

Greggory looked up as Brewer stormed through the door from the front of the shop. His eyes were wide, he breathed hard and his hair was a jumble. He ran to the table with the stacks of trimmed bills and picked up $1,000 worth. Then he shouted.

'Money, all this goddamned money! We're rich, at least we will be when we get this passed. Damn, but I feel rich already.'

Greggory stopped counting the bills and stared hard at Brewer. This guy could sink the whole operation for them. They had brought him into the deal so they could use this place out here in the wilderness.

'Look, Brewer. I have time to say this just one time. Now sit your ugly self down and listen to me like your life depends on it. This little game we have going is called beat the sucker for the bucks. We pass some store owner a counterfeit ten and get back eight or nine dollars in change. We pretend it's an ordinary buy, nothing more. We don't get excited or nervous or go wild. It all has to be routine, every day making boring purchases. We play it low key all the time. You understand? This is the toughest part of the operation, when we rake in our money. Real money. You mess up here and you go to prison for ten years. I go down, the press goes down, and maybe even Chicago goes down. I can't let that happen. If I thought you were going to screw up, I'd put a bullet right between your squinty little eyes right now. Understood?'

Brewer sat there nodding as Greggory talked.

When Greggory stopped, Brewer looked up. 'Yes, I do understand the seriousness of the operation. I'll not do anything to compromise it in any way. And I know the penalties. I am a lawyer. When I'm on the road I'll be the absolute low-key, friendly traveler who needs some small items and buys them, pockets the cash and walks out. I have five completely different outfits. Most with a hat, some with eyeglasses, one even in work clothes. I understand. We just about ready to wrap this up and get moving?'

'We ride out in the morning. We'll go early before most folks are up. You'll go south and I'll head for Bellville about twenty-five miles mostly east of here. The man at the post office said there's a stageline that comes to a dead end there. From there I'll move east. You go south and head for Randall and Jamestown if it's still there. Then on to Concordia. Don't pass any bills until you hit Concordia. Then get rid of five or six if there are that many stores you can buy something under a dollar, and ride out on the stage the next morning.'

'I know, I know. You think I'm a jackass the way you keep explaining things.'

'Better a live jackass than a dead one or one in prison.'

'Yeah, OK, I see your point. How do we split this up and how do we carry the bills?'

When it was done, they each had 250 of the bills, and they packed another 500 in a sturdy cardboard box, double-wrapped with paper and tied with string to send to Chicago.

'Two hundred and fifty bills will fit in your saddle-bags easy,' Greggory said. 'As soon as you get to a town with a stage, sell the horse and saddle, buy a small valise, and put your clothes in it from the sack you have tied behind your saddle. Then hide the bills in the valise. Remember, be a man who nobody notices. Don't dress flamboyantly. You have to vanish in a crowd, be inconspicuous. And for heaven's sake, be sure to keep the good money separated from the bad. All the good money will be in fives and ones. The counterfeit is all tens. Can you remember that?'

'There you go again, Greggory. You make me sound like a nincompoop. I'll get the job done. And who put you in charge here, anyway?'

'OK, I'm a little tense. Always get this way before I start the passing. Not my favorite part of the game but it's got to be played. You bought a horse down at the livery today and got a saddle and gear?'

'Right. I'm all set. Even some food in case I don't hit that first town before dark.'

18

During the week that Brewer and Greggory passed the counterfeit bills Wade had been busy. One night he slipped up on the roof of Anderson's house and stuffed an old blanket down the kitchen chimney, sealing it off. The next morning when Anderson made the breakfast fire the wood-burning stove gushed out smoke inside the kitchen so thick he had to rush his whole family out of the house. It took him an hour to figure out what had caused the smoke in the house. When he found out he knew that someone had deliberately put the blanket in his chimney. He wasn't sure who.

The next night Wade slipped into Anderson's back yard and worked loose the nut-and-cotter pin holding the right front buggy wheel on the axle. In the morning Anderson started for work, but drove only half a block. When he turned the corner into Main Street the wheel rolled right off the axle and dropped the buggy sagging hard to the front and right. The axle dug into the street dirt. The horse stopped and Anderson crawled off the rig, his face purple with fury as he shouted a string of obscenities into the air. He walked a half-block down the street where the steel-rimmed spoked wheel had rolled and pushed it back to the rig. Two men came along and helped him lift the right front end of the buggy to get the wheel back in place. He was an hour late opening the store and half a dozen customers chided him about it.

At the livery that morning Wade put on two new shoes for a town man's horse, then wandered up and sat near the mercantile. Yesterday people had been calling Anderson Mayor Smoky. Today the term had changed and they teased him about having a smoky wheel. Wade grinned. It was fun, but it didn't answer the ultimate question.

What was he going to do about killing Anderson?

His inability to come up with some satisfactory solution to the Anderson problem led him to think about Brewer. What could he do to the lawyer and print-shop owner? He heard about the new press that the wagon had brought down from the railroad. A rough journey. A man came with the new press, evidently a printer by trade. Lately the CLOSED sign had been on the printing shop's front door. Why bring in a new press and then close the shop?

Maybe the new man was learning how to use it. Then for the past week he had noticed that the law office run by Brewer was also closed. Nobody knew where he was or where he might have gone. That in itself was a bit unusual. Most always everyone knew everyone else's business and personal life in a town this size.

Brewer, who had stood by while his mother was killed and had shot his father, was his new target. What would be a just end for the man? He could confront him in his office, make sure he knew who he was, and what was going to happen. Then take him out the back door to a pair of saddled horses and ride due west into the farm and ranch country. Then, well out of town, he would make the killer beg for his life.

It didn't seem like enough. He wanted Brewer to suffer more than just one fearful afternoon. Something rougher, meaner, something that he would go crazy over.

Could he harass Brewer until he became so unhinged that he killed himself? That might take weeks. Could he do it? The stuffed chimney wouldn't work. Brewer had a house but he ate his meals in the cafés. Probably never set a fire during the summer. He didn't own a buggy, so there was no way to do the wheel-off routine. He did have a favorite riding horse. A beautiful palomino with golden mane and tail and lightly colored body. She was his pride and joy, and he had Mexican-style silver works on his saddle and halter. That might be one idea.

That afternoon he saw the closed sign come down from the law office. The mission would begin tonight.

It was just after supper and a half-hour before dark when Wade slipped up on the house Brewer had taken over from the previous lawyer in town. It was larger than most and had a small barn in back and a fenced acre where the horse could run during the day. Every night Brewer put the palomino in a stall in the barn, gave her oats, and then brushed and combed her down.

Wade lay in some tall weeds thirty yards from the barn and watched Brewer come out of the barn and close the door. He walked to the house twenty yards beyond the barn, fronting on First Street. Wade rested his chin on his folded arms and waited. He had learned how to wait from his pa.

He watched the sun go down miles

and miles away across the Kansas plateau. East Bend sat at an elevation of 1,465 feet. Some called it the high plains. Flat as the inside of a skillet and in the summer twice as hot. In a few minutes it was dark and lights blossomed in the Brewer house. He must have lamps in four or five rooms. Might make him feel like he had company.

Two hours later, Wade had taken a small nap. He checked the star time and came up with about 9.30. He watched the last light in the house go out, came to his feet, and carried his box of goods with him. First he eased open the barn door. He had to open just half of it. Inside he lit a match to find the horse, backed her out of the stall, put on a halter, and led her into the darkness. He had picked the spot, about a hundred yards from the house where, beside a small stream, grew a group of common persimmon trees. He tied her there and hurried back to the barn. The structure was twenty yards from the house. He spread the gallon of kerosene around the inside of the barn and over two bales of hay that had been broken open. Then he lit two matches and dropped them on the kerosene. It flamed up at once after a small whoosh from the vaporized petroleum. He saw it burning good and closed the barn door the way it had been. Then he ran from the barn a hundred yards down along the street but not near any other house. He waited until the barn was fully engulfed in flames and the red tongues of fire sprang out of the roof.

There had been no movement from Brewer. He ran to the front door and banged on it. He pounded it a dozen times until he heard a voice from the upstairs window.

'Hey, stupid, it's late, what do you want?'

'Your barn is on fire,' Wade screamed in a voice the lawyer could never identify. The shadow at the window vanished, the window clanged shut, and he heard heavy steps charging down the stairs inside. Wade took off running into the darkness of the night.

Brewer surged out the back door as Wade figured he would. Wade circled around so he could see Brewer in the firelight. Quickly a half-dozen men had gathered around, watching the blaze.

'Too late to save her,' one man shouted over the crackling and roaring of the fire.

'Get your mare out of there?' another man asked.

'Noooooooooooooooo,' Brewer screamed. 'Goldie is still in there. Got to get her out.' He ran for the barn. One of the men caught him and held him.

'Nothing is still alive in there by now, Brewer,' the man said.

'If Goldie was in there, she's dead. Didn't hear any screams from the horse. You know how they can scream.'

Two men held him now and Brewer broke down and sobbed. He dropped to his knees and pounded the ground with his fists.

The barn roof collapsed then in a shower of sparks and smoke. Soon the sides fell, one inside, another one outside scattering the men and boys who had come out to watch the fire.

By that time there were fifty people standing around in the edge of the firelight. Not much this exciting happened in town. Wade walked up to the edge of the crowd and asked whose place it was. They told him.

One woman shook her head. 'I'm next-door neighbor down about half a block or so. He loved that horse. She must be gone now.'

Wade waited until the last wall fell and heard the oohs from the crowd. Then he walked back to the Nelson boarding house. With daylight Goldie would be in plain sight from any room in the rear of the Brewer house. Brewer would cry himself to sleep tonight. Tomorrow morning when he found Goldie he would wonder who had burned down his barn but only after taking out the horse.

* * *

The next morning Wade had finished breakfast at the boarding house and was walking toward the livery when a man stopped him.

'You that farrier guy?' the man asked. He was a towner, with a black suit, a string tie, and a black, low-crowned Stetson.

'That I am, Wade Tretter.' Wade held out his hand and the man shook it.

'Ivan Hoff. Just got into town two days ago and I've been busy. But I have a mount that needs some looking at. I know you're not one of them vets but figured you might help.'

'Is she limping and clodding around?' Wade asked.

'Yes, that's it. Just a little limp but like she doesn't want to take another step.'

'In the livery?' Wade asked. The man nodded. 'Let's go take a look if you've got time.' He did.

Wade showed surprise at the condition of the horse's hoofs. Three were so overgrown that the shoes hardly connected with the ground. The fourth was in better shape but the shoe itself had broken in half.

'How long since you've tended to her hoofs?' Wade asked.

'That the problem? Great. You can fix it? I thought I might have to buy a new horse.'

Wade measured the hoofs, gave the size to the owner, and told him to go up to the mercantile and bring back four shoes. Wade began cutting down and shaping the hoofs. He had a lot of cutting to do. The work kept him busy for almost an hour, then the mount was properly shod and ready for a gallop around town.

Just as he finished he saw a rider coming on a beautiful palomino. He recognized the horse as it came in, and Brewer stepped down. He yelled at Old Gus.

'Hey, you worthless old wrangler, get out here and let's do some business.'

Old Gus came out of his small office grinning. 'Told you that you'd come back to me,' the livery man said. 'Same deal as before. Not a penny less and you pay extra for the oats like everybody else.'

'Yeah, yeah, all right.' Brewer stroked the horse's long neck and rubbed her ears. 'Make sure you don't rent her out while I'm not looking.'

'Hear you lost your barn,' Old Gus said.

'Some no-good burned it down but took Goldie out first. Now who would do a thing like that?'

'Somebody who hates you but doesn't hate horses.'

'Probably.' He pulled a folded wad of bills from his pocket and started to take one off, laughed softly, and put them away. From his other pocket he pulled out three one-dollar greenbacks and handed them to the livery man.

The owner of the horse that Wade had just shoed came up and checked the hoofs.

'You do much riding you should check the shoes every six months,' Wade told him. 'Even if you don't ride her much the hoofs are going to grow out.'

The rider paid him the two dollars and rode off toward Main Street.

Brewer was in a talkative mood. Old Gus stood and listened.

'I nearly died last night but two guys stopped me from rushing into my barn. I was damn certain that Goldie was in there burning to death. All night I wanted to kill somebody. Then this morning I looked out the kitchen window at the still smoking barn, and across the field I saw Goldie tied up in those persimmon trees.

'I let out a yell they could hear in Concordia and rushed out there. Never so glad to see that horse in my life. I mean, I came back from total despair to roaring happiness in an instant.'

'Damn, Brewer, you even talk like a lawyer.'

'Yeah, well, who knows, I might not be a lawyer all my life.' He grinned at the livery man. 'A dollar a week for pasture and the oats. That was our deal.

Oats three times a week. Holding you to our verbal contract.' He looked at his watch. 'Hey, I'm late for an appointment.' He handed the reins to Old Gus and marched up the street toward his office.

Wade watched him go. It was a small matter, but it would be an irritant. A beginning. The man he thought he had an appointment with wouldn't show up. Wade knew because he had left a note on the lawyer's door that morning asking for a ten o'clock meeting 'It's about an important land deal I want to make here in town. See you then.' He had signed it Johnson Merriweather.

Now that he was concentrating on Brewer new ideas came to him for Anderson but he shunted them aside, or adapted them for Brewer. He didn't care which one he disposed of first. He took his two dollars, waved at Old Gus. and walked the block to Main Street.

He should keep some pressure on Anderson. A little old-fashioned blackmail might work about now. He turned into the Mercantile and waited until a shopper had left with a half-pound of number ten box nails.

'I don't want you around my store, Tretter.'

'I can understand that. There is one good way to keep me away. That's to make me a loan of, say, two hundred dollars. You shouldn't have any trouble raising that kind of cash. Do you keep it here in the store or in our town bank?'

'Why should I give you two hundred dollars?'

'You know exactly why, you Missouri killer, you killer of women and wanton marauding murderer.'

'I wondered when you might think of money as a solution. I can give you a hundred and fifty. I was about to take it to the bank.'

'No, two hundred. Dig it up from somewhere. I want it now.'

'I could have you arrested for extortion, blackmail — '

'And I can have you arrested for multiple murders. What's your choice?'

He shook his head and went to the counter. Wade was beside him with his Colt in his fist and the muzzle aimed at Anderson. 'Just don't grab that revolver under the counter or you're a dead store-owner. The money, quickly, before a customer comes in.'

Anderson slowly took an envelope from a folder and counted out the $150. There were two twenties, but mostly they were tens and fives. Then he frowned. He dug into his pocket and came up with a twenty, then he found three tens in another pocket. He put them all together.

Wade moved Anderson's hands, took the money, folded it, and pushed it into his pocket. He ordered Anderson to walk with him to the front of the store, getting him away from his weapon. At the door Wade grinned at the frustrated store-man and slipped outside.

He laughed at the sour expression Anderson showed. Tough. Wade would deal with Brewer first. Wade had made it a habit lately to stop by the library on mornings after his work at the livery, and talk to Becky for just a moment right outside the front door of the library. He was obeying the letter of the agreement with the Lewtons. He had been to three courting times with Becky now, and had become friends with her younger brother, Tad for Thadius Lewton. While they talked a moment, Mrs Lewton hurried up to them.

'Inside, Mr Tretter. I need to talk to you right now.' It was plain to him that Mrs Lewton was worked up about something. Becky looked at Wade, lifted her brows and shrugged. They went into the library and to the far corner. Mrs Lewton shook her head.

'I don't know how to say this, so I'll just say it. Tad wants to talk to you. He says he knows something that is very bad and he doesn't want to talk to me and he won't talk to my husband. Tad is so upset about it that he threw up. I'd appreciate it if you could come over to the house right now and talk to Tad. We have to learn what this is all about.'

19

The three of them hurried down the boardwalk in front of the stores, then into the dirt of the street, across it, and down two blocks to the Lewton house. Mrs Lewton had a firm set to her chin that Wade had not seen before. She was either angry or frightened. What would young Tad Lewton have to tell him that he couldn't tell his mother?

Becky got to the front door first and held it open as her mother marched inside, then Wade held it for Becky, who gave him a perfect smile as she entered.

Inside they found twelve-year-old Tad sitting on the sofa reading a book. He jumped to his feet as soon as they came into the room.

'Just Mr Tretter,' Tad said.

Wade nodded. 'Why don't we take a walk?' Tad bobbed his head.

Wade looked at Mrs Lewton, who agreed.

Tad waved at Wade, leading him through the house and out the back door. The creek was 500 yards away and Tad didn't say a word until they came to it. Tad sat down on a flat rock and threw pebbles into the three-foot-wide stream.

'You anxious for school to start?'

'Not really. Summer is for fun.'

'Something must not have been fun for you recently. What was it?'

'The camping trip we took to learn about the woods.'

'When was that?'

'We just got back this morning.'

'Who went?'

'Our Sunday school class. Eight boys and our teacher.'

'Sounds interesting. What happened?'

'That's what I couldn't tell my mom. Our teacher is fun and likes to teach us about the woods and camping. We went out to Devil's Canyon. I don't want to get into trouble.'

Wade frowned. The boy was shaking. He was afraid of something.

'No, Tad. You won't get in trouble. If something bad happened, you need to tell me. What happened?'

'We were coming home and had to cross a narrow trail near the canyon. It dropped off a long ways on one side. Some of the guys didn't want to go across. The teacher laughed at us and called us cissies and little girls. Finally he yelled at us and we went across. Billy Smith tripped and fell over the side. It's a long way down. He didn't move after he hit the bottom, just lay there.

'The rest of us made it and then our teacher went down to help Billy. He stayed with Billy a while then came back up and hurried us the last five miles into town. We left Billy out there. I . . . I think he is dead.'

'Did your teacher tell the sheriff about it?'

'Don't think so. He said none of us should tell anyone what happened. It was an accident.'

'When did you get back to town?'

'About an hour ago.'

'Who is your Sunday school teacher?'

'Mr Anderson, the new mayor.'

Wade scowled. 'OK, you go back in the house and wash your face and then take a nap. I better go tell the sheriff. Billy might not be dead. We'll go look for him.'

A half-hour later, the sheriff, Wade and two other men rode out to Devil's Canyon, about five miles from town. They went to the place Tad had told Wade about and saw the crumpled body far below. It took them a half-hour to work their way down to Billy. He was dead. Wade guessed that he had died in the hundred-foot fall to the rocks below.

'It's Billy Smith all right,' the sheriff said. 'Old Terry is going to be furious. Let's get him out of here.'

They took turns carrying the body, after moving down the gully a half-mile to where they could climb out of it. Then they rode back to town with their silent burden.

Within fifteen minutes of their arrival in town half the people knew what had happened.

The riders took Billy to his parent's home, a small house at the edge of town where Terry Smith had a huge garden and sold vegetables in the summer. He worked part-time at the tin shop in town. He came to the porch, saw his son in Wade's arms and ran to him.

'My boy. Is he hurt bad?'

'Terry, he had a fall out at Devil's Canyon. I'm sorry, but he died out there.'

'No. It can't be. They were with their Sunday school teacher. They were safe.' He shouted the words, caught Billy away from Wade and ran toward the house with him. The sheriff followed.

'Terry, it was an accident. Not Billy's fault. Nobody's fault. It just happened.'

Terry Smith turned and glared at the sheriff.

'It was somebody's fault and I'm

going to find out who it was. Now leave us alone.' He went in the small house and slammed the door.

The men watched him go inside.

The sheriff nodded. 'Yes, give him some time to burn off the anger and fury. I know Terry. A quick temper, but he's pretty solid. I think it will be all right.'

Wade had his doubts. He'd seldom seen anyone as furious and worked up as Terry had been.

The sheriff frowned. 'I better go see Anderson and get his story about what happened. From what you told me, Wade, it seems like it was an accident. But what I'm worried about is why Anderson let the kids cross that trail? It's dangerous. Almost everyone goes around the long way when they are out there. We'll see what he says.'

Wade went to the Lewtons' house and told them what had happened. Little Billy was dead and his father was angry.

'Sheriff thinks that Terry Smith will

be able to deal with it. Don't be surprised if the sheriff comes by to talk to Tad. I'm sure he'll want to talk to several of the boys to tie down exactly why they were going across that dangerous trail.'

Wade said goodbye to the ladies and hurried then to check the livery. He had two more customers.

After supper at the boarding house he went down to the biggest saloon in town, the Lucky Dice, and got into a game of five-cent-limit poker. Tonight he paid more attention to what the other players did on the draw. He won two dollars, then lost that and wound up even for the night except for the two beers.

He felt strangely relieved and for an hour or two he couldn't figure out why. Then it hit him. He might not have to shoot Anderson after all. From the look on Terry Smith's face, Wade had the impression that Terry wasn't going to let Anderson get off with just an apology. It would be a wait and see situation. In the meantime, he could concentrate on Brewer.

He went back to his room and tried making out a list on Brewer. It didn't work any better than had the list on Anderson.

* * *

The next morning at the livery he had no customers. He went by the library, but Becky didn't come out. He stepped inside and called. The librarian, Mrs Young, hurried up, her eyes red, her nose running. She touched a handkerchief to her nose and shook her head.

'Becky isn't here. I found this note stuck in the front door when I arrived about five minutes ago.' She gave him a piece of paper with writing on it. The message was printed with a pencil in block letters.

BECKY HAS BEEN KIDNAPPED. BRING $500 TO THE DESERTED FLORENCE RANCH SIX MILES

NORTH OF TOWN AT NOON TODAY. DON'T TELL ANYONE ABOUT THIS. COME ALONE. BECKY IS FINE. KEEP HER THAT WAY BY BRINGING THE $500.

The note was not signed.

20

Wade read the note again and looked up to see tears coming down Mrs Young's face. He put his arm aroud her shoulders, took her into her office, and helped her sit down.

'I'll put out the closed sign. Don't worry, Mrs Young, I'll find out who has Becky and bring her back. Don't tell anyone about this.' He folded the ransom note, put it in his pocket, went out the front door, flipped the OPEN sign to CLOSED, and then ran down the boardwalk toward the livery.

He had Betsy saddled and ready to go in five minutes. He borrowed a rifle from Old Gus, and a dozen rounds to fit it. Then he rode on the north road, going as fast as he could urge Betsy to run. He galloped her for a quarter mile, then walked for a mile, then cantered her for another mile. He circled around to the left of the ranch well before he could see it. He wanted to be the first one there. He wasn't sure whether the kidnappers would be there by now. If he came in from the back they wouldn't be watching for him from that direction. He wondered how many men there would be. Two or three, he guessed.

He would be hunting again. Just like hunting wild turkeys in Missouri, only these turkeys were smarter and they could shoot back. He'd move slowly, cautiously, never making any noise or attracting attention. If the kidnappers were already there they must have left town right after they took Becky. Not likely. When he came to the back of the ranch, he was a half-mile from the buildings and on a little rise. He pulled up, stepped off his mount, and watched the buildings. He saw no movement. He looked at the place a small section at a time. There was a ranch house, a barn with half the roof fallen in, an outhouse, and what he guessed was a bunkhouse. In back of the barn stood the remains of a corral and beyond that a fenced pasture of about ten acres. A small spread.

When he was sure he couldn't see any movement he rode slowly forward at a walk, half-expecting a rifle shot to come from the old ranch house.

No shots came. He found an open shed behind the house where he could hide Betsy. He rode her in and tied her. Then he went inside and to the front of the house. A broken-out front window commanded the view down the wagon road into town. He would be able to see anyone coming from a mile away.

Why kidnap Becky Lewton? It wouldn't be for the money. The ransom was not big enough. So why? He had it figured out half-way to the ranch. It was a way to get him out of town and kill him. There would be a man with a rifle, or maybe two or three men with rifles, and they would try to punch several holes in his skin at vital spots. The kidnappers would come early and try to set up an ambush. They would bring

Becky with them to be sure he saw her. They could leave her on a horse tied to a tree in front of the ranch house. Her hands and feet would be tied. Then they would set up a crossfire. The only man in town who wanted him dead was Rudy Anderson.

Wade checked his pocket watch again. It was only half past nine. He had some waiting time. He cleared the rest of the broken glass from the front window and bellied down on the floor. The window frame was just high enough at the bottom to give him a firm place to rest the rifle barrel as he sighted in on the kidnappers. Would they come? Yes, they had to if they wanted their money. Would they let him ride into the yard and try for the exchange? Not a chance. If he had ridden in at noon he would be a buzzard's lunch before one o'clock.

He checked his watch again. Now it was 9.34. He pushed the watch deep in his pocket and vowed not to look at it again for at least an hour.

Less than an hour later he saw a small trail of dust down the wagon road. Four hoofs didn't kick up much dust, but four mounted horsemen would. Would he cut and run if four of them came, all with rifles and pistols? No. He could cut down two of them by surprising them before they could find cover. Then the odds would be two to one: not at all bad. They would have to attack him.

He didn't want to think where Becky would be during the gunfire. Out of the way, he hoped.

Twenty minutes later he could tell there were three riders coming up the north wagon road. One had to be Becky. As they came closer he saw that Becky was in the middle, her mount's reins tied to the saddle of the man riding in front. The second man came behind her.

When they were fifty yards away he saw that both the men had rifles in scabbards. They rode straight in, confident that they were the first to arrive. Wade grinned and began tracking the lead man. When they were in past the barn and twenty yards from the house, he refined his sight on the man's chest and fired. The round ripped through his shirt and skin and blasted a hole an inch wide through the kidnapper's heart. He slammed off the horse which bolted and ran straight ahead, jerking Becky's mount along with him. She screamed and held onto the saddle horn with both hands as the horses galloped past the ranch house and out of sight.

The second rider had slid off his mount on the far side the moment he heard the shot. There was no chance for Wade to shoot him. He walked his horse toward the low, one-story bunkhouse ducking down behind her. Wade still had no shot. He saw legs now and again, but not long enough to shoot. He'd pushed in a new round and now waited his chance. He should shoot the horse in the head, then nail the man as he ran. But he couldn't kill the animal.

A moment later the man darted away from the horse and through the bunkhouse door. Wade had sighted in on the door and waited, but his round was a fraction of a second too soon and high hitting the top of the door frame. Then the kidnapper was inside and out of sight. At least he didn't have a rifle. It was on the far side from where he had slid off his mount.

How to dig him out? Wade put two rounds through the open bunk house door, then stepped through the empty window frame and watched the bunkhouse. It had only one door that he could see. There were two windows on this side, both broken out and, he guessed, two more on the other side. He glanced over at the form lying in the dust. He hadn't moved. Dead as a stepped-on June bug.

Wade ran to where he could see the far side of the bunkhouse. A man had one leg out one of the broken-out windows. A snap shot from the barely aimed rifle hit the roof of the bunkhouse but drove the man back inside.

'You in the bunkhouse. Come out and I won't kill you. Otherwise I'll hunt you down like a rabid dog and kill you dead.'

His only response was a revolver shot from the nearest window forty feet away. The round dropped short, but Wade backed up another twenty feet. He shot through the nearest window, knowing the man had left that spot, but it would give the kidnapper something to think about.

Wade looked in the direction the horses had bolted. A runaway like that could keep going for a mile on nervous energy alone. He had to settle with this one first. Or did he? Becky could be in serious trouble out there. He made up his mind instantly and rushed for the back of the ranch house and his mount. He could find Becky and come back and chase the kidnapper.

He raced out of the shack behind the house and headed north. His eyes scanned the plains ahead of him. Nothing. No horse, no body, no two horses. They were tied together.

He rode at a hard gallop for a quarter of a mile to the top of the small rise. Then he stared downward at the slope ahead and saw something just beyond some trees. Could it be her? He raced Betsy again and she gave no indication of being tired. After 200 yards he caught himself and slowed her to a canter. Then he saw them.

The two horses stood together a quarter of a mile ahead. Both had their head down grazing. Becky sat in the saddle where she had been tied. She heard him coming and turned and cried out.

He was to her in a minute. He cut her bindings and hugged her to him while they both sat on the horses.

'Thank God you're alive,' he said.

'I'm fine now that you're here. I was frightened. They said they would kill you and then kill me and leave us out here for the buzzards and the wolves.

We don't have any wolves around here.'

He laughed at her denial of the wolves. His laugh came as a release of his tensions. He untied the reins from the second horse, and held them.

'We have to go back to the ranch house. The second kidnapper may still be there. I need to find him to learn who paid them to do this.'

'Oh, they told me. It was Mr Anderson. They said it didn't matter if I knew, because I could never tell anyone. That's when I really got terrified.'

They rode up the slope and he watched the land in front of them. The second kidnapper might lie in wait for them somewhere, behind a shrub or in a gully, and shoot them down before they knew he was there. He still had his six-gun, and by now he would have claimed his rifle. That thought made Wade stop. They were still almost a half-mile from the ranch house. Too far for a rifle: 880 yards.

'You stay here. Do you want to get

off the horse and sit on the ground?' She nodded. He helped her dismount. Then he gave her the reins of the two horses. 'Hold them here. He still has a rifle. I need to see if he's still down there.'

Wade rode off quickly before she could stop him. He went around to the west side and came in almost behind the barn. If the kidnapper had planned to gun him down from the ranch house he would be surprised. Wade made it to the old barn and dismounted. He took the rifle and edged around the rotting wood of the barn. He came where he could see the dead man. There was no horse in the ranch yard.

No horse.

Did that mean no kidnapper? He could have hidden the horse and waited for them. Or he could have ridden off and considered himself lucky to be alive. It took him a half-hour to clear all the buildings on the ranch. There was no hidden horse and he found no kidnapper. He gave a sigh of relief and galloped north for Becky and the two horses.

They rode back to the ranch, where Wade picked up the dead man and hoisted him over the horse's saddle. Then he used the lariat on the saddle and tied the man's hands and feet together under the mount's belly.

'We're taking him back?' Becky asked. She shivered. 'I've never seen a dead person before. Well, except at a funeral. He's really dead?'

'Hasn't moved for two hours and he has a bullet through his heart. I'd say he's pretty much dead.'

They rode for town.

* * *

Three miles ahead of them the other kidnapper, Delbert Greggory, hurried his horse toward East Bend. He was still furious with Anderson for talking him into this fool's mission. It had problems all over it from the start. The kidnapping was simple. They grabbed her on her way to the library, left the note, hustled her out of town down an alley, and then into the country. They waited for four hours in the shade of some blackjack oak trees near a small stream well off the north road.

The other man was the gunsharp. Anderson had found him in a saloon last night. He'd just ridden into town and for fifty dollars agreed to kidnap the girl and kill the person who came for her. He could also keep any ransom money brought. Greggory was along as insurance and to be sure that Wade Tretter was dead. They knew he would be the one to come to rescue his girl. Everything had gone wrong. It was a scramble. He thought he was a dead man finding Tretter with his rifle against a six-gun. Then Tretter had turned and ridden off to find the girl. His lucky break. He kicked the mount into a faster pace. He hated coming out here in the country on a kill job like this.

He had just come back from his road

trip with over $1,200 in good as gold US greenbacks. He would be a rich man in a few months. If Anderson caused any more problems, he was going to have to cash in. It had been a while since Greggory had killed a man, but Anderson would be no problem at all. He'd enjoy it. His usefulness to the team was over. Now he had to get back to town and work up an alibi for where he'd been all morning. He wouldn't have a problem with that. He'd taken to doing some printing for the locals. That would do it. The counterfeits were all out of sight, hidden away, and the plates were hidden best of all.

* * *

Wade brought them into town after circling around so he could drop off Becky at her house. 'Send Tad down to the library to tell Mrs Young that you're safe and sound,' he told Becky. She nodded and rushed into the house.

Wade led the horse with the body on

it through Main Street and had quite an audience when he stopped in front of the court house and called to the sheriff.

Engleright came out of his office growling but stopped when he saw the body.

'Who is he?' the sheriff asked.

'Never seen him before. He and another man kidnapped Becky Lewton. The other one got away. Becky is back home safe. You have any wanted posters on this man?' Wade gave the sheriff the ransom note.

The sheriff turned the dead man's head and stared at his face.

'Don't recollect nobody with an ear half shot off like his is. I'll check my Wanteds. Take him down to the undertaker. Then come back. You shot him?'

'Right. Self-defense.'

'Be some paper for you to write out. No charges on you.'

The story of the kidnapping and Becky's rescue spread all over town faster than Wade could walk from the livery back to Mrs Nelson's boarding house. She was full of questions. So were the men at the supper table. He told the story again, then said it was nothing any of them couldn't have done, and begged off on the game of checkers. He told them good-night and went up to his room.

He checked over his valise. He'd need to get Mrs Nelson to do some laundry for him. Under his shirts he found the packet of money. The $200 he had blackmailed Anderson for. That could be the start. No, as of Saturday, Anderson could be in trouble about Billy Smith's death. Have to wait and see. The district attorney might charge him with something. Probably not, Wade decided.

He took out the bills and counted them, then sorted them into stacks of twenties, tens and fives. He had the most fives. He lined up the bills and pushed them all together. For a moment he couldn't get the edges of them even. He looked again. The three ten-dollar bills were just a thirty-second or so of an inch larger than the other bills. Strange. He'd never seen that before. He took the three tens out and laid them side by side. What a pretty bill. Almost new. Pictures and numbers and tens all over it and a serial number.

When he first learned about money he had been amazed that the government had a printing press that would print all those bills and put a different number one each one. He looked at the numbers on the tens. The first one was: K38476838A. He looked at the second one. It was close to the first one: K38476838A. That couldn't be right. It looked like the same number. He moved one bill close to the other one so the numbers were near each other. They were exactly the same on two of the bills. The press must have made a goof that day. He checked the third bill. The same identical number.

Wade sat back and stared at the bills. They felt like good money. They were printed well and the figures were all right, except for the three identical serial numbers.

Wade looked through all the rest of the bills. None of the twenties had the same serial numbers. None of the fives did either. Just the tens. He'd heard of men printing up their own money. Counterfeiting they called it. He knew exactly where the bills came from. Rudy Anderson had passed them to him as real currency. The next morning he was going to talk to the banker. He had never met the man but he would know about counterfeit money. Where did Anderson get it?

21

The next morning Wade went straight to the bank. Closed. The sign on the door said it would open at ten. He checked with Old Gus but there was no farrier business waiting for him. At the library Mrs Young said she had sent Becky home to rest up and to get over the terrible scare of the kidnapping.

Wade had a cup of coffee at the Kansas Café as he waited for the bank to open. He worked on a refill on his coffee before the clock on the wall told him it was ten o'clock.

In the bank he asked to see the president. A woman led him into an office at the side of the lobby where the nameplate read: Archibald S. Marshall, President.

Marshall even looked like a banker. Dark-green eyes stared up at Wade.

'Mr Marshall, I'm Wade Tretter.'

'Yes, I've seen you around town. You're good with the horses.'

'Thank you. I have a problem.' He took out one of the ten-dollar bills and handed it to the banker. 'Is this real money?'

The banker held the note up to look through it at the light, felt the paper. Then he pulled a ten-dollar note from his wallet and compared the two. At last he nodded. 'Looks good as gold to me.'

Wade handed him a second bill. 'What about this one?'

Again the banker went through his routine and nodded. 'Looks good to me.'

'Compare the serial numbers on the two bills I gave you.'

The banker put them one next to the other. He frowned. 'I'll be horn-swaggled. I would have bet the farm that those bills were genuine. I was wrong. That's the one thing a counter-feiter can't change, the serial number.'

Wade gave him the third bill. 'They are also just a smidgen too big. You agree that they are counterfeit?'

'I do and I'll have to make a report to Washington DC.'

'Before you do that let's go talk to the sheriff. Maybe we can find out where the bills came from and who made them.'

The banker squinted and nodded slowly. 'Yes, yes, good idea. Then if we find out I can file a report and close it with the capture of the wanted men.'

Sheriff Engleright was not a happy lawman that morning. One of his best deputies had quit and his wife kept nagging at him to buy her a better kitchen range that had an oven. He looked up in surprise when the banker and Wade walked in.

'Morning, Mr Marshall, Mr Tretter. Why am I honored?'

'Counterfeiting,' the banker said and spread out the three ten dollar notes.

The sheriff went through his usual routine when checking for bogus bills. He finally rubbed the bill between his fingers and nodded. 'Look good to me,'

Sheriff Engleright said.

'Check the serial numbers, Sheriff,' Wade said.

'Oh. You're right. The numbers are the same. So they got to be counterfeit. Where did you get them?'

'I received them yesterday from our esteemed mayor, Rudy Anderson,' Wade said.

'Usually they buy a small item and try to get change. Marshall, you check your cash at the bank from yesterday to see if you had any more of these?'

'We checked every ten-dollar bill in the bank. They all were good money.'

'Where would Anderson get counterfeit bills?' the sheriff asked.

'I have an idea, Sheriff,' Wade said. 'Recently the lawyer here in town, John Brewer, bought out the local printer. Then a short time later Brewer evidently bought an expensive and high-quality printing press in Chicago and sent it by train into Nebraska, then down to our town by mule-drawn wagon. I'm wondering why a small town like East Bend needs a high-quality, expensive platen press like Brewer bought? Yes, one of the men in town who used to be a printer told me the press was extremely expensive but exceptionally good. The press is good enough to print these bills. Then the last connection is that Anderson and Brewer both rode in the Rebel army during the war. They are still good friends.'

'So let's go pay Brewer a visit and tear his place apart,' the sheriff said, standing and pulling on his gunbelt with its long-barreled .44 revolver.

The banker shook his head. 'Ten years ago, maybe. But these days the circuit court judge would throw out any evidence you found without a search warrant.'

'Damn them lawyers and their newfangled laws.'

'This one has been around for a hundred and fifty years, Sheriff,' the banker said.

The sheriff sat down hard on his

chair. 'But even ten years ago we didn't have to pay so much attention to them. Man was guilty he was guilty and we hung him.'

'Yeah, times are changing, Sheriff. So we need a circuit court judge.'

'Right. Where is that schedule he sent?' The sheriff pulled some papers off his desk, looked under a book and at last found what he searched for.

'Yeah, right. Judge Landower should be in Scandia today, tomorrow and the next day. Why three days in that little jerkwater place?'

'When does he come here?' the banker asked.

The sheriff looked at the schedule. 'Not for ten days.'

'These guys could be in Denver by that time,' Wade said. 'How far is Scandia?'

'About twenty-five, maybe thirty miles north and east.'

Wade considered it. 'I can ride up there, Sheriff, if you give me the statements and evidence that the judge needs to sign a search warrant. If I leave right now, I can be up there before dark, get the judge to sign the papers, then ride all night and be back here by eight or nine tomorrow morning.' He grinned. 'Then I'll sleep all day.'

'You'd do that?' the sheriff asked.

'Yes sir. I think one of these two men tried to have me shot twice and missed. Then one of them kidnapped Becky. I'd love to see both of them sent to the state prison for twenty years.'

The sheriff chuckled. 'Righteous anger is always good. I can have you two men's statements, and I'll throw in my own observation of the bogus bills and we'll send two of them along as evidence as well. I can have you out of here in fifteen minutes. First give me your statement about what you said about the press and its quality. Then you best go get your horse ready and take along enough water and some travel food to keep up your strength. Now let's get that statement of yours ready.'

Twenty minutes later Wade stepped out of his saddle in front of the sheriff's office. He'd told Becky and Mrs Nelson that he'd be gone for a couple of days, but he'd be back. The sheriff had the material ready in an envelope, which was closed and had a wax seal on the flap.

'You get that to Judge Landower and I guarantee that he'll have you heading back this way within ten minutes. He likes to move fast. Good luck, young man.' He looked at Wade again. 'Say, young Mr Tretter. How would you like to be my deputy? I just lost a man. Only three of us. I could use a go-getter like you around here.'

'Let's talk about that when I get back,' Wade said.

Then he rode. The directions were simple. He went over open country north about six or seven miles until he came to the cross-state wagon road. When he found the wagon trail he turned right and picked up some speed. He paced Betsy all morning. He figured he was doing an average of about five miles an hour. He was ten miles out and twenty to go. Just after his noon meal of dried apples, some jerky and a big drink of water he passed a small community called Courtland. Then it was a long stretch that a sign said was eighteen miles on to Scandia. He let Betsy walk for an hour and then lifted her into a canter. He paced himself with chaws on the salty beef jerky and drinks from his canteen.

Just before five o'clock he came into Scandia and asked at the sheriff's office where he could find the judge. They told him court was out for the day and the judge would be either at his hotel room or at supper at the Square Deal Meal restaurant. He found the judge working on an apple cobbler dessert in a booth by himself.

'Judge Landower?'

The judge looked up, his frown showing his irritation at being bothered during his supper. He stared at the trail dust on Wade's clothes and face and nodded.

'Looks like you did some riding to find me, boy. What do you need?'

'From Sheriff Engleright down in East Bend. He sent me with some evidence asking for a search warrant to nail these guys.'

The judge looked at the envelope and the seal.

'Put it right there, son, and I'll get to it in ten minutes. A man can't rush his apple cobbler and the cigar that comes after it. Why don't you use the time to get yourself some supper?'

Wade went outside, found a horse trough, washed off his hands and face, and slapped the dust off his pants and shirt.

Back inside he ordered stew and ate quickly as the judge finished his coffee and the cigar. Then the judge opened the sealed envelope. He read the statements, fingered the counterfeit bills, then looked up and waved at Wade.

'Yes, counterfeit, no doubt, but

excellently done. The only give-aways are the serial numbers. Who caught it first?'

'I did, your honor.'

'Good work. I'll give you a handwritten court order authorizing a search for counterfeit money, and any apparatus and materials needed to produce same including paper, ink, and a press. That should do it. Oh, the search is for any printing plant or office and the named parties' residences.'

He waved Wade away and took out fresh paper, pen, ink well, and began writing.

Wade used the time to order a piece of pie and coffee. When the judge finished he folded the paper and motioned to Wade.

'That should do it. It will stand up in any court in the state, especially in my court. You in a rush to get back, I'd guess.'

'Yes sir.'

'You come up here on one horse thirty miles?'

'Yes sir.'

'I'd suggest two horses to go back. Ride one and lead the other one for an hour. Then change mounts and ride for another hour switching back and forth until you get to town. This way you can keep up a canter most of the way with a few gallops thrown in.'

'A good idea, your honor, but I don't have enough money with me to buy — '

The judge waved him to silence. 'Forget it, the livery man here owes me ten years of his life. I'll give you a note. He'll give you the horse and you can send payment back in the mail. No nag out there he has is worth more than twenty dollars. Have him throw in a saddle and bridle as well. I'll put that in the note. Now, good luck. And I'll see you in court in ten days or so.'

* * *

Four hours later, Wade was surprised how much land he was covering. He figured he must be making close to six miles an hour. At this rate, he should be back in East Bend well before daylight. It had been almost eight o'clock before he got things straightened out with the livery man. He snorted at the letter from the judge. Said he doubted he'd ever see the twenty dollars but had to do it anyway. Wade had promised to pay him with a bank draft.

Now at midnight, Wade figured he had covered about eighteen miles. Ten or so to go. The small town of Courtland should be coming up soon. Then it would be only eight miles into East Bend. The two-horse system had worked out extremely well.

He arrived back in East Bend without any problems and put the two horses away in the livery without waking Old Gus. He slipped into the boarding house only to find a suspicious Mrs Nelson with a four-pound iron frying pan aimed at his head. She stopped short.

'Oh, Wade, is that you?'

'Truly, truly, Mrs Nelson. Don't swing that frying pan.'

'Long trip?'

'I've just ridden sixty miles and I'll pay for it dearly tomorrow. But it's for a good cause.' He had brought back the evidence with the search warrant. He went up the steps one at a time, shuffled into his room and got the lamp lit, then he pulled off his boots, pants and shirt, and dropped on his bed. He went to sleep before he remembered to blow out the lamp.

Mrs Nelson promised to awaken him at eight o'clock in the morning and she did, by rapping on his door.

Wade called out and sat up groaning. Every bone in his body was on fire and every muscle was trying to tear itself into pieces. By the time he got to the sheriff's office just past 8.30, he felt better. He put the envelope down on the sheriff's desk and told him about the trip, the extra horse and how somebody had to sell the horse and send a check back to the livery man in Scandia.

The sheriff only nodded, read the search warrant and called to his deputy.

'Business,' he said. 'I want you to bring Mayor Anderson down to the print shop, right now. Mr Tretter here and I will go ahead of you and hope to surprise Brewer and that new pressman hard at work.'

They took the court order and walked half a block to the print shop. The door was locked. The sheriff patted the search warrant and kicked hard at the lock. It jolted and unlatched and the door swung inward.

'Hey, what the hell?' a voice called out. The two men rushed inside and found Brewer at his desk.

He looked up from the desk at the side of the office section of the shop. Wade darted through the curtain into the back and saw a man heading for the back door. Wade drew his Colt and sent a round into the wall just in front of the runner.

'Hold it, right there,' Wade bellowed. 'Or the next round goes right into your spine.'

The man turned. He was the driver, the pressman. Wade didn't know his name. 'Back to the office,' Wade said. Wade marched him into the front of the building. The sheriff had Brewer handcuffed and now he put a pair around the other man's wrists.

'Greggory, isn't it?' the sheriff said. 'We have a search warrant and I'm putting both of you under arrest for counterfeiting. You want to tell us where the bogus bills are, or do we tear this place apart one board at a time until we find them?'

Before they could answer, the door opened and Mayor Anderson and the deputy came in. Anderson saw the two men handcuffed and turned to the sheriff.

'What is this, Sheriff Engleright?'

'We've just found out these two men are part of a counterfeiting operation run from right here in town. We thought you as mayor should know about it.'

The merchant's eyebrows lowered and he frowned.

'Sheriff, I'm shocked. I had no idea these men were doing anything like counterfeiting. Have you found the money yet? What denomination are the bogus bills, twenties?'

22

'Actually the bills are the ten-dollar variety,' Sheriff Engleright said. 'I wanted you to know about it, Mayor Anderson, so you could warn the other merchants in town not to take any ten-dollar bills with this serial number.' He had it written down and handed it to the merchant.

'Right, I'll be sure to tell everyone in town.' He looked at the two manacled men and shook his head. 'What a shock, I never would have suspected. At least you've nipped the problem pretty near to the bud, or at least let's hope so. I better start making the rounds.' He nodded at the sheriff.

'Sheriff, did you have a chance to go over that material I left with you about life insurance? I'm an authorized Pennsylvania Life Insurance agent like I told you. I have a thirty-thousand-dollar policy myself. We talked about a ten-thousand-dollar policy for you. To protect your wife and children in case anything happened to you.'

The sheriff shook his head. 'Haven't had a chance to talk it over with my wife yet. I'll let you know.'

The mayor nodded and went out the door.

'That liar,' Greggory whispered.

'What was that, Mr Greggory?' the sheriff asked. 'I'm not sure I quite heard you.'

'Didn't say a thing,' Greggory growled.

Sheriff Engleright shrugged. 'No matter. Let's get started tearing this place apart until we find any already printed notes, the paper and ink needed, and most important of all, the engraved plates they were printed from.'

They worked through the small office, looking in every drawer, a filing cabinet and an assortment of boxes stashed in a closet and others on the floor.

'Nothing,' Wade said.

The deputy watched the two arrested men while the sheriff and Wade went into the back and started searching. There were dozens of boxes of paper. Some were on racks against the wall. Engleright looked at it and shook his head. He went back to the office and told his deputy to take the two prisoners to jail and lock them in, then bring back the other deputy and they all would search.

Wade worked over the boxes on a shelf and the far side of the building for a half-hour. He found nothing to connect the men with the counterfeiting. He checked the press and found traces of fresh green ink that matched that on the bills. He told the sheriff and they worked harder.

Something bothered Wade and it took him another half-hour to figure out what it was. Then he had it. This had to be Saturday, still. It was the longest day of his life.

'How is Terry Smith holding up?'

'Mad as hell, but his wife is helping to keep him busy so he doesn't do anything rash. I think he's over most of his rage.'

* * *

The four of them worked the rest of the morning searching the back shop, hunting for the money, the plates, the paper and the ink. At noon they went to the cafe for a quick sandwich, then they were back at it.

About two o'clock one of the deputies found some paper he thought was suspicious.

'Could be,' the sheriff said. 'A bill is supposed to be twenty-five per cent linen and seventy-five per cent cotton. This sure feels like linen in there.'

Wade found a box under a section that was all covered with dust, except for one stack of boxes. He moved the clean boxes one at a time but found nothing until he opened the bottom one.

'Hey yeah!' Wade shouted. 'I've got them, at least some of them.'

The others came to look. There were stacks and stacks of neatly banded ten-dollar counterfeit bills.

'A stack like that is a hundred bills,' the sheriff said. 'That's ten thousand dollars' worth. Must be near a thousand bills in this box. A thousand bills would be ten thousand dollars worth of counterfeits.'

He told the two deputies to continue looking for the rest of the money, the ink and any stash of real money. Then he took the box and went back to the office with Wade.

'Oh, yes. Now we have it. Enough to put these guys away for a long time. It will have to go to a federal court, I'd guess. Judge Landower will know about that. Sure won't be any bail.'

In the sheriff's office they put the counterfeit money in the safe and both grinned. Wade told the sheriff that he was going back down to the print shop to do some more searching.

In the print shop Wade worked through the stacks of paper and boxes for another three hours. They found the green ink, and later in a hollow-sounding section of the floor, one of the deputies located a heavy metal box. When they got it open they saw stacks and stacks of real greenbacks and the two engraved plates.

'Must be two thousand dollars' worth in there,' one of the deputies said. 'All are fives and ones. Must be the change they got when they passed one of the tens.'

Wade went to the sheriff's office with the deputies. They took the engraving plates and cash, and waited while the sheriff counted it. He signed off on the amount, so there would be no mistake. It would be taken to the bank on Monday and put in a special holding account. It was still Brewer's money.

Wade took a quick trip to the Lewton house. It was nearing five and he wanted to tell them about Brewer's and Greggory's arrests.

'Just as soon as the sheriff finds him, he's arresting Anderson as part of the counterfeiting,' Wade told Mrs Lewton and Becky.

'Good. It's strange what some men will do to make money.'

Wade made it just in time at the boarding house for supper. He'd never eaten goose before but a flight had landed in a field south of town. Mrs Nelson's hunter friend bagged two of them. The one they had roasted and which now lay half-carved on the table must have weighed thirty pounds.

'You'll be eating on this one for three days,' Mrs Nelson told them. 'I have ways of cooking it so you won't ever know.'

After supper Wade walked down to the livery and asked Gus if Rudy Anderson had been there.

'Now how in the world would you know that?' Gus asked. 'Yeah, about a half-hour ago he rented a horse and said he wanted to take a ride to calm himself down after the counterfeiting scandal. He took off south at first, riding easy.'

Wade ran to get Betsy out of the corral. He had a bad feeling that Rudy would run. He had everything to lose by sticking in town. It was his Rebel Raider mind-set again. Hunt, take, kill and run.

'He have any traveling gear with him, like a bedroll and a food sack?' Wade asked as he saddled Betsy.

'Not a bit. But he could stop by his house.'

Wade rode hard for the place he had been told was the Anderson home. It was a little after six o'clock so there was an hour and a half of daylight left this time of year. There was no horse in front of the house, nor one at the back door. He continued almost out of town, rode up a little grade, and looked south. Where would Rudy go if he headed south? Wade had no idea. He scanned the one wagon road leading south but saw no rider. Then, to the left, a hundred yards off the road, he saw a white horse and rider. Gus said Rudy had asked for his favorite white mare and saddled it.

Wade kicked Betsy in the flanks and aimed her at the rider. If he couldn't catch Anderson before dark, it would be ten times as hard to find him tomorrow with daylight.

Wade figured he was a mile behind Anderson. Even if Anderson didn't know he was being chased, it would be almost impossible to catch him before dark. A flat-out gallop from Betsy could last only a quarter of a mile then she would have to walk. Anderson hadn't been doing much riding lately so he probably wouldn't try to ride all night, even as scared as he must be.

A fire? He doubted that Anderson would stop and build a fire. He must know about how that would pinpoint his location. So what did that leave him? Wade worked it over in his mind as he rode. The country here was fairly open, with cattle scattered around. A ranch house here and there but not many. He would keep away from them. The road? He would get back to it for easier riding. But would he ride after it got dark? Wade guessed that Anderson would ride no more than an hour after dark and that he would be on the south road.

A half-hour later, almost at dusk, he saw Anderson move back to the trail of a wagon road and ride on.

Wade spotted a small creek going under the road about the place where Anderson rode back on it. That would be his landmark.

Then it was dark. He rode on, coming to the creek. He took out a match and checked his pocket watch. Just eight o'clock. He would ride for an hour then a half-hour more down the road. By then he hoped that he would have passed a sleeping Anderson well off the road.

If he was right he would be in a concealed position in the morning at daybreak, and would wait for Anderson to ride by. Wade had his Colt and a borrowed rifle from Gus. He was ready. He could take Anderson in dead or alive. The sheriff would be glad to see him in either state.

23

Wade had slept little that night and he was fully awake with the dawn. He had moved twenty yards off the road into a small thicket of brush and trees. With light he could see a half-mile down the wagon road in both directions. So far no sign of the merchant. Wade had a long drink at a nearby stream then saddled Betsy and ground-tied her in some fresh grass.

He waited in the brush out of sight of the road.

* * *

It was nearly an hour before he caught sight of Anderson coming toward him on the road on his white horse. When Anderson was twenty yards away down the road Wade fired a rifle shot into the road in front of him and bellowed out his orders.

'Hold it right there, Anderson. Not a move or you're a dead man. Stop, now.'

Anderson gave a long sigh and pulled the mount to a halt.

'Now ground-tie the nag and get down slow and easy on this side of the horse. Do it.' Wade waited for the man to get down.

'We know all about your tie-in with the counterfeiters. Your friends have been talking like crazy. But you'll never stand trial on the charges. Not a chance you get off that easy. If you have a hideout derringer, drop it on the ground.'

'No gun,' Anderson said.

Wade took Anderson and the two horses well off the little-traveled road into a heavy stand of trees and tied the merchant's hands and feet. Then he cut a four-foot-long stick with a fork on the end and went hunting. He had to turn over a dozen rocks and logs before he found what he wanted, a four-foot-long rattlesnake. He wasn't sure what kind it was, but it was angry. He nailed its head to the ground with the forked stick then picked it up holding it just behind the head. The tail thrashed around but wasn't dangerous.

He showed it to Anderson who shivered and looked away.

Wade laughed. 'Afraid of snakes, Anderson? Good. The time has come for justice. Remember Missouri, bloody Missouri they called it. Where you rampaged and raped and murdered innocent men, women and children? Yeah, you remember. So meet your jury, judge and executioner. Me? No, not me; Mr Angry Rattlesnake here. He's the one.'

'For God's sakes, Tretter. Don't do this.'

'Sure, just like you didn't shoot down my pa in cold blood and let your man murder my ma. Now shut up your face.'

Wade led Anderson to a flat place covered with grass. He pushed the merchant down on the grass and got a large rock from the stream. He had cut stakes from nearby brush and now spread-eagled Anderson on his stomach on the grass and tied down his hands and feet to the stakes driven deep into the ground.

He had tied the snake by the tail to a tree. Now he brought it up and showed it to Anderson again.

'Your good buddy, Anderson. You'll get familiar with him quite soon.' Anderson lay with the side of his face on the grass. He lifted it and shouted at Wade, spouting obscenities.

Wade snorted. 'You have only yourself to blame, killer of women and children.'

Wade took the snake and another stake, stout cord, and tied the rattler to the stake, which he drove into the ground. The snake rattled and slithered toward the first target he saw, Anderson. But the man's head was out of reach.

'Now our little game is this, Anderson. Mr Rattlesnake here will be tied just far enough from you so he can't strike your head. That is unless you don't hold it up as high as you can from the ground. The minute you relax and let your head fall toward the grass, you'll be in range and our friend here will nail you with three or four strikes. Interesting, no?'

'Tretter, for God's sakes. You can't do this. This is murder and you know it. I can't bring your folks back but this is torture.'

'And about time, you murdering maniac. About time you suffered the way I have for the past five years. Now hold your head up, I'm giving Mr Rattler here a little more slack in his tie-down. Just enough to reach you if you drop your head.'

'You can't do this, Tretter.'

'Watch me . . . for as long as you live.'

Wade waited until Anderson lifted his head high then loosened the cord and let the snake move toward the closest danger, Anderson. It had to stop just out of reach but with enough space to strike if the head came down. Its tongue darted out and back, its tail rattled, and Anderson screamed until his throat was raw and his voice tailed off into a vacant whisper.

'Tretter, no. Pull it back. I can't hold my head up for long.'

'So sweat, killer. Remember how many people you killed in Missouri just before the war ended. Think about that, you murdering animal.'

Tretter moved back ten feet and watched the drama unfold. He thought he would enjoy seeing this killer meet his fate as he should. But he had pangs of regret. Still, the man deserved to die. He had killed twenty, maybe thirty innocents. It was justice. Wade had figured that he couldn't just shoot Anderson and bring back his body. He was running from a counterfeiting charge, not murder. So he had come to the idea of the snake. He would say he followed Anderson and found him dying from snake bite near his fire. The evidence would be plain on his face.

The merchant was stronger than Wade had guessed. It was almost fifteen minutes before he dropped his head. The snake lunged forward but with no coil to propel it, he missed the sweating head. Anderson screamed and jerked his head back up.

'He missed me, Tretter. See that. I win. He doesn't get a second chance, right?'

'Wrong, Anderson. You didn't give my pa no second chance.'

Anderson bellowed in fury and rage. His head lowered a fraction of an inch and he powered it back up.

Wade watched Anderson sweat. He was through with shouting obscenities now, saving his strength to keep his head up.

Then it happened so quickly Tretter almost missed it. Anderson's head came down and hit the grass, the rattler struck, pulled back and struck three more times. Each time the sharp fangs dug into Anderson's cheeks, he screamed. Then the snake pulled back. Anderson lay there writhing in imagined pain. The venom hadn't started to do its work yet.

Wade knew the best thing to do for a rattler bite was to keep the victim as quiet as possible. Any activity would increase the spread of the venom through the bloodstream. Anderson might have known that too. He quieted. Wade went up to him and cut the bonds on his hands and feet. Anderson sat up, saw the rattler still tied and screamed in rage. He jumped up and leaped ahead stomping on the snake with his town shoes, suffering one more strike on his leg before he had killed the rattler.

'Well, Anderson, that evens things up. The snake is dead. Now all you have to do is run back to town and get the doctor to save you. Go ahead, run, you murdering beast.'

'You won't shoot?'

'No. Go. Run.'

Anderson looked at him a second

then screamed in protest and started running back toward town.

Wade watched him go, then picked up the reins of the two horses and followed. Anderson made it almost 200 yards before he stumbled and fell. He got up and tried to run again but staggered to the side and fell again. This time he couldn't get up.

Wade walked up near him, ground-tied the horses, then sat down six feet from the Missouri Border Raider.

Anderson looked up, sweat and tears staining his face. 'Help me, Tretter. Get me back to the doctor.'

'I'll help you the way you helped my pa. My guess is that you have maybe a half-hour to live yet.'

Anderson struggled to sit up. He stared at Wade for a moment then looked away. 'How did they catch the bad-money scheme?'

'You did it, Anderson. You gave me three of the counterfeits, those three tens you gave me as part of the two hundred. So the whole thing is your fault. Should make you die happy.'

Wade watched Anderson's eyes glaze over. His head shook and he rubbed his eyes. Wade wasn't sure just how rattlesnake venom killed a person. It might slow down and stop the lungs from working or it could attack the heart. He had no problem letting Anderson die now that he knew about the life insurance policy he said he had. A policy worth $30,000 meant a fortune in a time when the average working man made from $300 to $500 a year.

He'd heard all sorts of stories about snake bites. He'd never watched a man die from one before. Until now.

Anderson struggled to stand, took three steps then stumbled and collapsed on the grass again. He stared at Wade. 'You monster, you devil, you demon.' His words were slurred now, his eyes going wild; he had been slouching on one side, now he rolled on to his back. His eyes were pleading now.

'Back there in Missouri. That was

war. Told you that. War. We did bad things in war.' His voice had faded to a whisper. The left side of his face where he had been bitten had swollen up to twice its normal size.

Anderson kept talking but his voice was almost gone. Wade couldn't understand a word he said. His head lolled to one side, then came straight, then back again. For the first time, Wade realized the man's breathing was short and labored. A moment later he gasped for breath. His hands came up to his chest then fell away. His eyes fluttered, then a long whoosh of air came out of his mouth and his head rolled to one side.

Wade felt a tear roll down his cheek. The man was dead. It was the hardest thing he had ever done. Rudy Anderson had paid the final price for his murderous deeds. The slate was wiped clean. Captain Brewer would get his justice over the next twenty-five years as he served his prison term. For just a moment, Wade felt total relief. It was over. The vengeance trail was finished.

Now he could get on with his own life.

* * *

It took him half the day to ride back into town. He created a stir when he led in the white horse with Anderson's body tied over the saddle. He stopped in front of the sheriff's office and went inside. The sheriff listened:

'I figured he'd run. He was in it up to his eyebrows. I chased him. Caught him this morning. Looks like he got bit at least four times by a rattler. He killed it but it was too late. Terrible thing to be killed by a snake bite. He suffered a lot before I found him. By that time there was nothing I could do.'

* * *

Three days later the sheriff hunted up Wade at the livery.

'Got me a favor to ask you, Tretter. You heard about Brewer and Greggory getting held over for trial by the circuit judge and him sending them on somewhere to a federal court for trial. Anderson met his fate a little early for my liking. But we're not going to worry about that. Anderson's passing leaves the county a good-sized problem. A week ago the county assessor took over the mercantile for back taxes. I'm to hold a sheriff's sale of the property and stock within a month. Problem is, there are a lot of goods in that store our town needs. I want you to open it up and run it for the county for the next four weeks. Then somebody will buy it and you can work for them or go back to being a farrier.'

'I don't know anything about a mercantile,' Wade said.

'You're a fast learner. Here are the keys. Get right down there and open up and spread the word.' The sheriff paused. 'One more thing. I talked with Mrs Anderson. She's been all broken up about her husband. I asked her about the life insurance Rudy talked to me about. She said, yes, he did have a policy by his own company. She found it and it's for thirty thousand dollars. A lumpsum payment. The banker says she can invest that at eight per cent interest and have two thousand four hundred dollars a year to live on. More than enough for her to be more than comfortable for the rest of her life. Then too, she'll get the money from the sale of the store after the taxes are paid.'

'What if nobody buys it?'

'They will. Somebody always does. All they have to pay is the back taxes. In this case nine hundred eighty-three dollars and ninety-five cents.'

'That's all?'

'That's the minimum bid. For a store like that it might bring in five or six thousand dollars. The excess over the taxes will go to Anderson's widow to support her and her family.'

Wade took the keys. The mercantile had fascinated him. Now he could play there for four weeks. He'd get paid something for his work, but hadn't asked how much. Didn't matter.

He hadn't really thought much about it, but he had accomplished his task of punishing all four of the Rebel raiders. Three of them were dead and the fourth was looking at twenty years in some hell of a federal prison. His trip West had been a good idea. Now he even had a regular job running a store.

* * *

Four weeks later the sheriff had his sale on the steps of the courthouse. Only four men bid on the mercantile. Two were from out of town, and to his surprise one of the town men was Doctor Lewton. He won the bid at what Wade learned later was almost $4,000.

An hour after he'd won the bid, Dr Lewton came into the mercantile and looked around.

'Quite a place you've got here, Mr Tretter.'

'From what I hear it's your store

now, Dr Lewton.'

'Mine, yes. It is mine, but I'm no merchant. On the other hand you have a talent for this place. Everyone who has been in here has told me so. I want you to stay on as the manager. Then maybe in a year or two you might be in a position to buy me out.'

Wade laughed with embarrassment. 'Me a merchant? Never even thought about it. I'm a farrier.'

'You also broke up that counterfeiting ring right here in town, and you got Brewer sent off to spend twenty-five years in some dank federal prison.'

'Right, Dr Lewton. I did spot the fake money.'

'Like I said, a man's got to be more than a farrier if he wants to have a family. Needs something to support a wife and two or three young ones. From what my wife says, you and Becky seem to be hitting it off rather well.'

Wade felt a shiver shoot up his spine. 'Sir, does that mean that you agree that we can announce our engagement?'

'Now, let's see. You were a farrier. Now you're the manager of the largest store in East Bend with a promising future. Yes, I think that would help your chances. Of course I'll have to think it over for a time and see how you do here at the store.' The doctor took out his watch and lifted his brows. 'Time surely gets past us in a rush, doesn't it? I'm afraid I have patients waiting. Expect to see you at church tomorrow and then at the house tomorrow night. Why don't you come early about five and you can sit supper with us. Yes, I think that would be a good idea. You agree?'

'Be proud to come to supper, Dr Lewton.'

The physician nodded and walked quickly out of the store, setting off the small tinkling of the bell at the front door. It jangled again, Becky came running in and up the aisle, and grabbed him in a huge hug.

'Did he? Did he? Did he offer you the store?'

He hugged her, lifted her off the

floor, and twirled her around.

'That he did, young lady, but I'm just the manager.'

Becky kissed him hard on the lips to his surprise. 'You're coming to supper tomorrow night. Mother insisted that Father ask you. And I just know for sure that we're going to be able to be engaged after we eat.'

'Hey, I'm still just the manager here. I've got a lot to learn.'

'True, but I heard Daddy talking to the sign painter. Sometime tomorrow the old sign is coming down and the new one is going to go up that says Tretter Mercantile. It's our wedding present from Father. Isn't that wonderful?'

Wade could hardly believe his ears. She smiled that special smile where the dimples popped in her cheeks and nodded. He grabbed her, spun her around again, as he felt tears of joy stinging his eyes.